WORLD OF OUR OWN
and Other Stories

Stories from the second FEMRITE
Regional Residency for African Women Writers

Edited by Hilda Twongyeirwe

FEMRITE PUBLICATIONS LIMITED

FEMRITE PUBLICATIONS LIMITED

P.O. Box 705, Kampala

Tel: 256-041-543943/0772-743943

Email: info@femriteug.org

www.femriteug.org

Copyright © FEMRITE - Uganda Women Writers Association 2011

First Published 2012

ISBN   978-9970-700-24-0

Cover illustration by Bonnetvanture T. Asiimwe
E-mail: asiimwebonne@gmail.com

Printed by:

Good News Printing Press Ltd.

P.O. Box 21228 Kampala, Uganda

Tel: +256 414 344897

E-mail: info@goodnewsprinting.co.ug

Contents

Introduction

FEMRITE presents herein African women's voices, resulting from the second African Regional Women Writers' Residency held in January, 2011 in Jinja, one of Uganda's most popular tourist-attraction towns. The residency was attended by writers from six countries; Mamle Kabu: Ghana, Ketina Muringaniza: Zimbabwe, Wame Molefhe: Botswana, Maliya Mzyece Sililo: Zambia, Elieshi Lema: Tanzania, and from Uganda: Beatrice Lamwaka, Lillian Tindyebwa, Constance Obonyo, Elizabeth Namakula Lenana and Linda Lillian. In addition to the residency stories, the anthology includes submissions from other African women writers.

In order for one to qualify for the residency, one had to be working on a novel manuscript. The aim was to encourage and support women novelists. While it is easier to get the space and time to write a short story or a poem, it is much harder to complete a novel. As a result, only a few women in Africa are writing and publishing novels. One of the main aims of the annual regional residency is to get women writers on the continent to come together, compare experiences, share solutions and encourage one another to sustain longer writing projects.

This year, the programme consisted of skills enhancement through writing exercises, the discussion of novel manuscripts, literary presentations and, of course, private writing time. All this culminated in a public reading held at the Uganda Museum in the capital city, Kampala, where the writers in residency read extracts of what they had worked on. For some, it was the first time they read to such a large audience. There were also inspirational field excursions: a boat ride on Lake Victoria and a visit to Sipi Falls, one of Uganda's most spectacular waterfalls. During the ten days, participants shared personal stories, their fears and aspirations as writers, and their experiences as mothers, daughters, wives and professional women. People have several layers of lives and it takes certain comfortable and safe spaces to unpeel these layers so that the stories underneath can be shared. Such is the space FEMRITE envisaged in designing the Regional Women Writers Residency project. Indeed, one of the participants, Elieshi Lema from Tanzania, was moved to comment: "This is the first time I sit in a family of my writing sisters!" It is hoped that the annual residency will continue to strengthen sisterly ties among African women writers.

FEMRITE is very grateful to The Swedish Institute, The Commonwealth Foundation, UK, and Karavan (a Swedish journal of international literature), the three institutions that funded and supported the event. This is the second time that The Commonwealth Foundation has funded the Residency and accompanying publication and we appreciate this constancy. Karavan was enthusiastic about the regional residency and so not only did it support the programme, but joined FEMRITE as a co-host. Thus Birgitta Wallin, Eric Falk, and Kerstin Norborg, as well as Professor Gakwandi from Makerere University Literature Department, facilitated the program in Jinja. Swedish author Kjell Eriksson was also very instrumental, especially in the planning process as he was part of the team that visited FEMRITE prior to the residency.

Although participants Ketina Muringaniza, Wame

Molefhe and Linda Lillian are not represented in this anthology, FEMRITE recognises their valuable contribution at the residency. We hope everyone who reads World of Our Own and Other Stories will enjoy it as much as we did putting it together. The themes evoked in these stories are quite diverse; each story presents a world of its own, inviting readers to explore and excavate the secrets therein. FEMRITE is very grateful to all the contributors for their generosity of spirit.

Editor

Foreword

Reading and writing are inseparable. Writers always read, for pleasure like the rest of us, and to learn from others, compare themselves with them. They also read their own texts, again and again. Some readers claim that they do not write but that is true only in the strict and boring literal sense. They bring their own experiences and imagination to the story and so make up a great part of it.

Plato, the philosopher, feared the co-operation between writers and readers in the shaping of a story because he saw in it a dangerous unmooring of meaning. Without the guiding voice of the author to secure and explain their intentions, words were made to enter the world on their own and were easy prey to readers' whims. Written words, he said, were orphans.

What Plato really feared was the loss of control over meaning. He was afraid to let go and he spoke, of course, as a certain kind of anxious writer. There are many who do not share Plato's anxiety. The gaps in stories, the complexities of scene, the ambiguities in turns of phrase, and the things that happen when narratives travel are what keep readers interested, and what allow them to talk unendingly about literature. Those are the features that give readers right who lay claim to stories. Many of us say, 'This story is mine, I relate to it, I know that character, I have been in that world.' That world then bears our mark as well as the author's. Words in stories are not orphans; they belong to as many families as there are readers. For many writers in World of Our Own, unlike Plato, there is a certain joy to the unpredictable lives that their stories will lead in the minds of their readers.

Most of the authors presented in this anthology participated in the workshop FEMRITE and Karavan hosted in Jinja earlier this year, and a majority of the stories were either begun, or workshopped during the residency in Jinja. Our memories of those productive ten days – from the first breakfast to the last night's party – are vivid. For us Swedes, tormented at that time of year by cold, the climate – at times it was only slightly warmer than an ordinary Swedish summer's day – was like a long exhalation. For all of us, the lush, calm setting offered the necessary escape from everyday commitments.

The discussions of work in progress, which were a central part of the workshop, remain particularly bright in memory. Having a first audience at hand is a luxury not afforded by every writer, but here it was. Under the shade of parasols and thatched roofs, writers turned readers, and readers became writers, while the conversation meandered. Relaxed and informal, it was always focused, and the insights, the imagination and the rigour brought to these exchanges made them truly enjoyable. During these sessions, words were given temporary homes and the author was a guest invited to visit.

This anthology is testament to the work done during those days in January and February. It is a collection of great variety and multiplicity that now awaits its many-fold completion. That is the task of the readers. All the words in here are ready to venture out into the world on their own, and enter other lives – those of the readers.

Erik Falk and Birgitta Wallin, Stockholm August 2011

FEMRITE
Regional Residency
for African Women Writers

Butterfly Dreams by Beatrice Lamwaka *was first Published in "Butterfly Dreams and other short stories from Uganda" Ed. Emma Dawson (CCC Press, 2011), and is reproduced by permission. Was short listed for the Caine Prize for African Writing 2011*

Butterfly Dreams

Beatrice Lamwaka

*L*abalpiny read out your name on Mega FM. This was an answer to our daily prayer. We have listened to the programme every day for five years. You and ten other children had been rescued by the soldiers from the rebels in Sudan. For a minute we thought we heard it wrong. We waited as Labalpiny re-read the names. He mentioned Ma's name. Our village, Alokolum. There could not be any other Lamunu but you.

During the last five years, we had become part of the string of parents who listened to Mega FM. Listening and waiting for the names of their loved ones. We sat close to the radio every day. Our hearts thumped every time we heard Lamunu or Alokolum.

Without saying words for one hour and each day we sighed after the programme. When the days turned into years, we prayed more often. Your name seemed to have disappeared and our chance of seeing you faded. We waited. We bought Eveready batteries to keep the radio going.

1

Lamunu, we may never tell you this: we buried your *tipu*, spirit, when word went around that you would not come back to us. The neighbours had begun to tell us that you would never return. Bongomin, who returned after four years of abduction, said he saw your dead body bursting in the burning sun. We never believed you were dead. We also didn't want your *tipu* to roam northern Uganda. We didn't want you to come back and haunt us. Ma never believed for one moment that you were gone. It was her strength that kept us hoping that one day you would return. She said she dreamt that butterflies were telling her to keep strong. The night after the dream there were so many butterflies in the house. We thought she was running mad. We thought you had taken her mind with you.

Ma wore *opobo* leaves for three days to let your *tipu* rest. We knew that she did it to make us happy. We advised her to let you rest so that she could move on with her life. She never did. She walked around as if her *tipu* had been buried along with yours. Your *tipu* was buried next to Pa. We didn't want you to loiter in the wilderness in the cold. Ma said you deserved to rest. To rest peacefully in the other world. Then, we heard your name on the radio. And we didn't know what to do. Run away? Unveil your *tipu*? Let you go on without knowing what we had done? We may never find the courage to let you know this. Maybe one day you will see the grave with your name on it and then the butterflies will give us the right words and strength to tell you.

You were at World Vision, a rehabilitation centre for formerly abducted children. You were being counselled there. You were being taught how to live with us again. Ma cried and laughed at the same time. Yes, you were alive. We couldn't believe at long last our anxiety would come to rest. That night,

2

Ma prayed. We prayed till cockcrow. We were happy. We were happy you were alive. Pa might have turned in his grave. We were happy to know you were alive.

***

You returned home. You were skinny as a cassava stem. Bullet scars on your left arm and right leg. Your feet were cracked and swollen as if you had walked the entire planet. Long scars mapped your once beautiful face. Your eyes had turned the colour of *pilipili* pepper. You caressed your scars as if to tell us what you went through. We did not ask questions. We have heard the stories before from Anena, Aya, Bongomin, Nyeko, Ayat, Lalam, Auma, Ocheng, Otim, Olam, Uma, Ateng, Akwero, Laker, Odong, Lanyero, Ladu, Timi, Kati. We are sure your story is not any different.

When you returned home, Lamunu, we were afraid. We were afraid of you. Afraid of what you had become. Ma borrowed a neighbour's *layibi*. Uncle Ocen bought an egg from the market. You needed to be cleansed. The egg would wash away whatever you did in the bush. Whatever the rebels made you do. We know that you were abducted. You didn't join them and you would never be part of them. You quickly jumped the *layibi*. You stepped on the egg, splashing its egg yolk. You were clean. You didn't ask questions. You did what was asked of you. It's like you knew that you had to do this. Like you knew you would never be clean until you were cleansed. Ma ululated. You were welcomed home. Back home where you belonged.

We watched you silently. In return, you watched us in silence. We gave you food when we thought you were hungry. You gulped down the sweet potatoes and *malakwang* without

3

saying a word. We didn't want to treat you as if you were a stranger but in our hearts, we knew that you were new. We knew that you would never be the same again. We didn't know what to expect of you. We waited to hear you say a word. We wanted to hear your husky voice. Hear you do the loud laugh you did before the rebels snatched you from us. We wanted to tickle you and watch your body move with laughing. But you were silent. You watched us with awe. You had grown now. Your breasts were showing through the blue flowered dress that you wore.

We greeted you. We thanked God when we saw you. You didn't answer our greetings. You looked at us. We saw your eyes glistening. We knew you were happy to be back. We knew you were happy to see us alive.

That night Ma cried in her bed. She whispered your name time and again as if wishing you would at least say Ma. Although she was happy you were back, she never said it. She expected you to say something. Something that would make her believe your spirit was in that body you carried around. We wanted to know whether your *tipu* had been buried with your voice. We had never been taught how to unbury a *tipu*. We only hoped that your real *tipu* was not six feet under.

We wanted to see you alive again. Although you were fifteen then, we wanted to know if you were still interested in becoming a doctor. We wanted to see you smile again. We wanted to see your eyes brighten as your mother gave you water and did the dance that you liked when you were a child. We wanted something that would make us know that you recognized us. We wanted to do our best to make you happy.

Ma never spoke of the butterflies again. We never heard of the butterfly dreams any more. We wanted the butterflies to come and say something to Ma.

***

We watched you as you studied our new home. Our new home had become something new. We watched the neighbours watch you with disgust. They were not happy you were back. Some of them still clutched the radio waiting for Labalpiny to read their son's name. They waited to hear him call out their names like *lupok cam* call out our names to give us yellow *posho* and beans.

Lamunu, we no longer till our land. Our children no longer know how to hold a hoe. They have forgotten how the groundnut plant looks. Now, our land buries our children. Our gardens grow huts. We now live in a camp. *Lupok cam* call it internally displaced people's camps. From the sky our camp looks like a farm of mushrooms. We have empty huts with empty people whose *tipu* have been buried or have taken a walk.

Look at the huts, Lamunu. This is something that we don't expect you to understand. Something you couldn't recognize. This is something that we don't understand. This is our home, something that we don't know how to explain to you. Something we took refuge in. This is our home that keeps us alive. Keeps us sane. Just huts. Grass and bricks. Just huts to hide our nakedness. When Latim and his neighbours built their huts here, they said Alokolum was safe. Their children will not be abducted. Their wives will not be raped. They will have something to eat. Then so-and-so built in our gardens all with the same hopes and dreams. Then everybody wanted to build their huts in our land. We couldn't dig any more. We had no more food. We later learnt our home had been marked in the map of Uganda as a camp.

Don't look at us like that, Lamunu. Yes, we now eat yellow *posho*. Yes, yellow *posho* that Ma used to feed Biko, Pa's hunting dog, before the war. We wait for *lupok cam* to provide us with cooking oil and beans, and of course, yellow *posho*. That's all we eat now. Sometimes we don't have enough. Sometimes *lupok cam* don't even come at all. We scramble to get out of the camp to look for something to stop the gnawing feelings in our stomachs. Just a little something. Some wild plants. Some *malakwang kulu*.

Some things that our ancestors never ate. Then we found out there were soldiers guarding us. They don't want us to get out of the camp. Why? we asked. They said they don't want rebels to abduct more of us. These days, my dear, they abduct anybody. Anybody who they can force to stand and be shot in the battlefield.

We asked the soldiers, where were you when Lamunu was abducted. Where were you when the rebels came and took our young ones? Where did you go to when the rebels came and raped our women as we watched? They told us they had not been paid. Sod off! we told them. Let us go to look for food. Then they came with their sticks to beat us as if we were schoolchildren.

***

You spoke in your dreams. You turned and tossed in your mud bed. We held your hands. You were like a woman in labour. You spoke of ghosts. You spoke of rebels chasing you in Adilang because you tried to escape. You spoke of Akello, your friend, who they made you and your team beat to death because she tried to escape. You said you didn't want to kill her. You said you remembered the commandment 'thou shall not kill'. You said you didn't want to participate. You didn't want to hurt anybody. You said you saw Akello covered with sticks. You saw the blood in her mouth. You watched as the older rebels checked to confirm that she was dead. You were nauseated. You tried to vomit but there was nothing to let out. The last meal, raw cassava and boiled chicken, which you had looted from a camp, had already been digested.

We listened to you. We wanted to feel your pain. We wanted to know what you knew. We squeezed your hand. We wanted you to let out what you had been holding onto. You let us squeeze your hand. You didn't wince when blood flowed. We never could drain all your pain away.

***

Today, we watched you get drenched in the rain. You stood there still as the rainfall poured on you. You were not disturbed by the loud thunderstorm. We made space for you in the hut. Waited for you with warm clothes. We thought you were letting out something. We didn't interrupt you.

As the rain became a drizzle, you entered the hut. You bypassed Ma with the warm clothes in her hands. You sat with your wet clothes on. We noticed that it was the time of the month for you. You let the rain wash the blood away. You let us watch the blood streak down your leg. You didn't see the tears rolling down your mother's face.

7

Later that day, we listened to you curse under your breath. We watched you tremble when you heard the government fighting planes flying over Katikati. We knew that you were worried about the people you left behind. We knew that you knew what would go on when the planes went after the rebels. We didn't ask you for stories. We have heard the stories from Anena, Aya, Bongomin, Nyeko, Ayat, Lalam, Auma, Ocheng, Otim, Olam, Uma, Ateng, Akwero, Laker, Odong, Lanyero, Ladu, Timi, Kati.

***

Lamunu, we remember as if it were yesterday when the rebels came to our home. That night was the night we knew that there would be many more nights like that one. We heard the butts of the guns hitting people's heads. We heard the screams. We heard the rebels demanding our children from our own homes. We were helpless.

You were still dazed with sleep. One rebel not much older than you grabbed you by the hands. You were only wearing a t-shirt. Ma grabbed a skirt for you to wear. You went out of the house with it still in your hand.

Ma's pleas and cries were only answered with the butts of guns on her head. She asked them to take her instead. But the rebels demanded medicine. They wanted the medicine she brought from the government hospital in town. Lamunu, Ma would never have let you go. You were only eleven. Reading for your Primary Leaving Exams. You always wanted to be a doctor. You said you wanted to do what Ma was doing, not as a nurse, but as a doctor.

8

We later learnt that they went house to house in Katikati as well, taking all boys and girls around your age with them. They said that the rebels would train the children to fight. Train them to lure other children. Join the big war to save the Acholi. Oust the government. Overthrow Museveni's government. We didn't know what that meant. We didn't want to ask anyone. What we knew was that we didn't want our children to get involved in that war.

***

We watched as you always prepared to go to school like it was a special ritual. Brushing your teeth and then taking a bath. You carefully splashed the water from the *galaya* onto your slender body. You didn't eat the breakfast that Ma made for you. You packed it in your school bag so that you wouldn't be late for school. We admired you for that. Even when the war started and many children were waylaid, you managed to get there. You cursed the teachers and called them cowards when you didn't find any children or teachers. Days after a heavy fight between the rebels and soldiers you continued to go to school. You never gave up, even when you didn't find anybody there.

You said that the war only affected the education of the children in the north. The rest of the children in Uganda studied. And the exams were all the same. You went to school when everyone was hiding in the bush. Ma begged you not to go. Children were waylaid by rebels on their way to school, she pleaded. You always managed to get to school. Found an empty class. Disappointed, you would come home. Ma later became your teacher. Ma taught you about reproduction even

9

if she knew she shouldn't say such words to her daughter. You
were eager to learn. Pa wanted to teach you too, even though he
didn't know how to read and write.

***

Lamunu, we don't know how to tell you that Pa is no
longer with us. You may have noticed that he is not around.
We don't know with which mouth to tell you that he was cut
to pieces by those who you were fighting for. He was found in
a garden he rented in Lalogi. He said he could not depend on
Lupok cam to provide him and his family with food. You know
your father. He was a proud man. He believed that a strong man
should show his strength by the amount of food he had in his
granary. Before the war, there was a lot of food in the granary.
The neighbours were jealous of that. He dug like a tractor. His
cows were the best in Alokolum. Everybody wanted to buy
milk from him. Even the lazy Lutukamoi, he tried to dig night
and day but couldn't get done half of what your father could
achieve.

The rebels found him digging and asked him what he
was doing since everybody was supposed to be in a camp. He
said a man has to provide for his family. They mocked him and
told him to join them to fight if he was strong man. He said he
would not join them because he did not start the war they were
fighting. Ten young men beat him up with whatever they could
find. They later cut his body into pieces. Lamunu, we did not
eat meat after we buried your father and we have not eaten
meat since then... We could never understand why another
human being could humiliate another, even in their death.

10

Each day we pray that we get the strength to tell you. And one day when the war ends, you will tell us your story. And we will tell you our stories.

***

We learnt from the neighbours that you went to school. You asked the headmaster to register you as a primary six pupil. We didn't know that you could talk. We were happy that you said something, even though it wasn't to us. The headmaster looked at your skinny body. You told him you wanted to become a doctor. He asked you whether you could pay. You didn't answer that. You knew that we didn't even have a coin to put food on the table. You said you didn't care and that all you wanted to do was to study. You said you could pay when you were finished with your education.

You entered a primary four class. The pupils watched you silently. They thought you were a mad girl. They muffled their screams, worried that you would hit them or something. They knew that the war had brought something that they didn't understand. They wanted to survive, so whatever didn't kill them they would watch to try to find a way.

Ma ran to school when she heard that you were there and argued with the headmaster. She wondered why you didn't tell her anything. She wanted to help you. She wanted you to talk to her but she didn't want to push you as well. She loved you though she could not say it.

***

11

Ma spoke to the headmaster of Lacor Primary School. The headmaster agreed to let Ma pay your school fees in instalments. She said that she is happy that you still want to go to school.

You said *apwoyo*. You said thank you to Ma. That's the first word we have heard you say. We're happy to hear you say something. We hope that you will be able to say a lot more. Tell us more than Anena, Aya, Bongomin, Nyeko, Ayat, Lalam, Auma, Ocheng, Otim, Olam, Uma, Ateng, Akwero, Laker, Odong, Lanyero, Ladu, Timi... Most of all, we want to hear your voice.

***

You look very beautiful in your new uniform. The headmaster of Lacor Primary School for formerly abducted children has donated the uniform to you. Ma says that you will get special treatment. Most of the children are like you. They too have killed, tortured other children. They too fought in a war that they didn't understand. The teachers will treat you well, Ma says. They have had special training.

You are very happy. We can see you have woken up early. You have packed your bag with your new books. You have written your name neatly on the books.

We know that your dreams will come true. You will be a doctor some day. Do the work that Ma does but wearing a white coat.

There are tears in Ma's eyes. You look the other way. We know that you know they are tears of happiness.

12

Colour Separation

Mamle Kabu

August 13th, 9.30 p.m.

<u>Police Statement</u>

At 7 p.m. on August 13th, I was driving home from work on the Ring Road dual carriageway. It was raining and as I stopped at a red light, a car hit me from behind. My spectacles fell off my face from the impact but I did not sustain any physical injuries. However, my bumper and taillights were smashed. The other driver had obviously been going too fast considering the wet condition of the road. But when I confronted him he was not apologetic. While we were arguing, a policeman arrived on the scene. We both explained what had happened but he seemed to be more partial to the other driver's explanation.

So I slapped him.

#

August 14th, 1 a.m.

<u>Cockroach-infested cell, Nima Police Station.</u>

O*n August 13th at 7 p.m., I took the Ring Road dual carriageway to get home from work. It was raining hard. I stopped at a traffic light . . .*

Oh God, I can't do this statement! I thought it would help to practise on here but the problem is, whichever way I write it, I'm just going to sound so . . . *guilty.* I've never done this sort of thing before. Writing statements. Being arrested. Assaulting a police officer. Yes, it does look bad in writing, doesn't it? That's the problem with facts: putting them in writing is like casting them in concrete. They set like rock and weigh a ton. No more lifting them up to see what's hidden underneath. Better get on with it though because my battery will be running down soon. Had to bribe them to give me the laptop. Hope the rest of my stuff is safe. I'm just going to bash away until the battery gives out to stop myself going mad in this place. OK, here goes.

I was on my way home on August 13th at 7 p.m. . . .

No, this is just not going to work. Trouble is, there's no way I can write down what really happened. What *really* happened to me, I mean. It wouldn't make any sense to them. Probably not to anyone. Not sure how to explain it. And do they want explanations in police statements anyway? Don't they just want "the facts"? Dialogue is fact, though, isn't it? So how about if I write down the things they said. Like —

14

"Madam, am I responsible for the water on the road? Ah! Stop shouting at me like that. If you're angry, shout at God and tell him it shouldn't rain when you're driving."

Excuse me? You crash into me from behind at a red light and *you're* angry? I've never wanted to strangle a person so badly in my life. Can't write that in my statement though, can I? Or that I asked him if I was also supposed to ask God to pay for the damage to my car. Yes, that was what really set him off.

"White lady like you? God has already given you plenty money so why should you need more for this small thing?"

That was when the onlookers began to titter and the word "*broni*" started to pop up here and there. So he plays to the audience by switching into Pidgin English.

"*Fine, fine broni lady wey dey tell black Kofi broke-man like me say make ee bring moh-nay!*"

And the titters turn into outright laughter. He's loving it. He switches again, this time into Twi, for greater effect. Yes, I can write down what people said, but how can I explain the way it made me feel? I couldn't believe it. No, actually, I could. That was the sad part, being seen as the baddie just because of my colour, my difference. Yes, I knew that feeling, that kick in the guts, because I'd had it before.

But the crash must have jolted my brain, because for once in my life, I lost control of the feelings those words, those titters, those pointing fingers awoke in me. It was as if all the pain and rage that had built up over the years—trapped and tamped down by the need to fit in, understand, be tolerant—had been waiting patiently for this moment. Now, they burst out of their pressure chamber, burning up everything in their wake and blasting apart my normal, controlled self.

15

"How dare you?" I screamed, my voice seesawing hysterically, catching in my throat as I fought back sobs. I pointed my finger in his face. "You hypocrite! Trying to make me look bad when you know it was your fault."

Of course, I was only spicing up the drama, living up to my role and goading the audience like a good villain should. But this villain couldn't shed her costume after the show and with it, the jeers of the audience. Floating above the scene, my normal, level-headed self could only observe and shake her head as the policeman strode up. *Officious black policeman finds hysterical white female bellowing at innocent black male*, she noted.

After giving me a warning the policeman made a show of listening to the story. I mentioned that I resented the man's attempts to bring colour into the issue.

"So we shouldn't call you a white lady eh, madam?" His bullying tone softened in amusement. That spontaneous, cheeky humour I love in my supposed country people, but couldn't bear right then.

"No. Even if I were white, my colour has nothing to do with it."

"Anyway, it's true, you're right." He looks me up and down and nods his head wisely. Then he turns to the man and says, "Hey, my friend, can't you see this one is not white, she's red!"

Murmurs of realization, I-told-you-sos and the cognitive labels "half-caste" and "copper-coloured" float over from the roadside audience. Sometimes I find it cute, that total oblivion to political correctness. But not now. And my opponent, always ahead of the game, slips smoothly back into the male camaraderie of Pidgin English.

16

"True-true you dey talk, Officer. Some fine red woman wey dey vex for me serious like dis. Hmm, Officer, you sabe somtin? Like she no shout-shout ladat, she for sweet me paaaa! Eh, red woman!" he finished, turning to me with a wide smirk on his face.

And I go for him, like a mad bull in the ring after the very colour he is brandishing in my face. The policeman grabs my shoulders just in time and holds me away from the man. "Madam, I have already warned you. Ah! But what is your problem; he's just admiring your colour. If you don't take care he will ask you to marry him just now!" And he howls at his own wit. Till I almost knock his head off with a slap. He cries out in pain and I almost do the same at the stinging and swelling of my hand.

End of laughter. End of show.

And here I am. Me. In jail.

Crazy.

#

I'm not the only one around here who feels that way. All the other prisoners are shocked to see a 'white' lady in their cell. And they couldn't handle it when I started crying. The lady officer who brought me some drinking water said: "Oh, Madam, please. Stop crying like that. You're going to make me cry too." But I was on another level altogether, past caring what anyone thought. So far inside myself that I'd lost sight of my image in the relentless mirror of social scrutiny. My sobs came from that core, a universal language, instinctual and contagious.

17

"Madam," she repeated, troubled, "please give us a number so we can call your people to come and bail you out." I shook my head yet again, baffling her. "Oh, Madam, you can't spend the night here, a fine white lady like you!"

    "It's OK," I managed to say. "They'll come for me tomorrow."

Fine white lady. If it had been tongue-in-cheek I could have squared up to it, but its ingenuousness was more formidable by far. Where did one begin? For now I was defeated in the colour wars. She wouldn't understand anyway. Just as she can't understand why I haven't told anyone. In a way I'm glad that Joe is away and doesn't yet have to know he has a jailbird for a wife. And I don't want to alarm Mum and Dad either if I can help it. Besides, I wouldn't know how to answer their questions.

What got into you?

We've never really talked about it but I don't think they'd understand either. For Dad, racial discrimination only goes in one direction, and for Mum there's never been any problem. Yes, of course we're different, but we're accepted, welcomed, even admired. You can't blame Mum really, she and her international-spouse comrades. Women who have known disownment and vilification for crossing the colour line. Can't blame them for seeing acceptance in anything more subtle,, for staring right through the glass wall of their kids' identity crises and then searching for the problem when the kids can't get their lives together.

So, no, I won't be calling Mum and Dad just yet. And to be perfectly honest, I don't want anyone to see me like this. There's something I have to face up to in here tonight and I have to do it by myself. I've already called the house and told Akua there was an emergency at work and I had to take a colleague to the hospital and spend the night with her. I hope she can sell it to the kids somehow and settle them down for the night. I hated doing that but there's no way I can let them see me in such a state. For that alone, it's worth staying in this hellhole. I could hear the questions in Akua's voice, she knew something wasn't right. But it was, "Yes, Madam," as usual. Unlike the policewoman, who was more persistent: "Madam, I beg you, call and let them come and take you out of here, okay?" But in the end she shook her head and walked sadly away. I was too alone for her to reach me.

#

August 15th, 7.43 p.m.

Dear Julie,

Sorry, I know you're dying to hear the details, but I couldn't face talking about it yesterday. It was all too raw and I was still sort of gathering my thoughts. Hope you understand. I think email is easier for me right now. It's almost funny imagining your shock upon hearing that your sister assaulted a police officer and spent the night in jail. Road rage, gender rage, colour rage, all in one. Too much for me I guess.

OK, let's see how I can explain it. You've been a black woman over there for so long you've probably forgotten what it was like to be a white girl over here. But do you remember how you felt when someone shouted "nigger" at you on the subway last year? Well, that's kind of how I felt yesterday. And I don't care if they say it's different here, that it's not meant negatively. If we don't like colour labels over there, why should we like them over here? People here complain about getting racist treatment abroad, but they don't think twice about calling out "Broni" to a white person on the streets here.

19

And never mind that the slightest shade lighter than black is white. If we're lucky, we get red! Why is it that the one colour we really are is the one we never get called? Not white, not black, not red, not copper-coloured! Just brown . . . plain brown. As if it's not bad enough having an identity slapped on you like a label on a jar, it's not even the right one. Remember that little ditty the kids used to chant on the streets? I still get it all the time: "Broni! How are you? Ahm fine, tenk you!"

African children. Who are taught to call anyone older than themselves "Sister," "Brother," "Auntie," "Uncle," to keep their eyes and voices low when questioned by adults, to begin every sentence with "please." So then, what makes it OK to chant and point fingers and forget their manners? It's like being different changes all the rules. Like it means you don't need to be respected or you don't have feelings. Almost like it takes away your humanity. It scares me that colour is all it takes to do that.

But they don't mean any harm, I've been told, they're just kids, some people even find it cute. But, if they're just kids, where are the adults to teach them it's wrong? And as for cute . . . treating a person disrespectfully just because they're different can stop being cute in a hurry. And it has done many times. But hey, that's world history, these are just a few harmless kids right? And the worst of it — that every time people slap a colour label on you, they're saying the only part of you they see is the one that's different. So black people call you white and white people call you black and if you get dizzy and ask where the hell you're supposed to belong, then there's another label for you, you're a tragic mulatto.

Well, no need to go on; at least you're one of the few people who know what I'm talking about. Just had to get it off my chest, I guess. They dropped charges in the end and I was free to go, but you know something weird, sis? I'm glad it happened. Maybe I had to be locked up with myself to realize it but there's nothing tragic about being what you are if you know what that is and don't let others decide it for you. They'll tell you you're white because you're not black, or black because you're not white. But why do you have to be either when you're both and neither? Yes, that's an identity in itself, and an OK one too. And if you stifle it under one or the other, act like it doesn't exist, then you're denying yourself. Well, I for one don't need anyone to tell me what I am or what I'm not, because in that prison cell I finally found a home. Inside myself. My brown self.

Love,

Your colourful jailbird sister.

Endless Distance

Lillian Tindyebwa

*M*adam sits quiet. Ssebo too. I glance at them from time to time. I am dressed in a black *busuti* and a black head-dress like the rest of the family. I wish I could say something, a word, a phrase, an anecdote or a proverb; something to wipe the lines from the faces of Madam and Ssebo. Something to part their lips into a smile, even if it lingered for only a moment.

Madam always enjoyed the way I spoke. But would she now? I wondered. She always said I made her laugh with my ideas. She used to say I sounded prehistoric, talking of things which no longer worked. She would say, "Oh, Robinah, that no longer works," in that gentle but firm voice of hers. I remember when I told her I was going to put a string of beads around Pamela's waist. She was one year old. "What for?" Madam asked.

"Oh, it will help to shape her waistline and give her hips prominence," I explained.

"Ah, Robinah," Madam had said amidst laughter, "you are just living in your own world. People no longer do such things."

23

I remember, too, when she had the twins, I told her what she was supposed to do, but she did not take it seriously. She just laughed.

Now, Madam is so far away from me. I know it will be hard to get near her and Ssebo. They are surrounded by their friends, all big names in the business world, CEOs, managing directors, even cabinet ministers, all are here.

It is a funeral service for Hedrick, the younger twin. We are in a church at last but for a reason I would ask God to change. I wish Hedrick had been able to attend this church as a living person. But Hedrick never attended church.

I glance from Madam's face to Ssebo's, their swollen eyes staring at the flowers on their dead son's casket, and my mind is crammed with past dawns of the crying newborn and the sunsets of sending them off to schools in faraway lands. They were mine too. Hedrick was twenty-two; almost the same age Madam was when I first came to live with them.

The day I arrived, Madam was the only one at home. She welcomed me. Ssebo had gone to work; I don't remember if he had started these businesses that now take him away from home for long periods. I am sure he had not; he started travelling when the twins were five years old. I remember them fighting to sit on his knee whenever he returned from his trips. He would end up carrying both at the same time. The twenty-three years that separate now from then are just like a Book of Life to me.

Another thing I remember was the smile on Madam's face when she saw me that day as I arrived at her home. Oh, it was so warm; like the sun emerging from behind the clouds. It was the first star of the evening that tells you it is going to be a good end to your day. My worries disappeared. You see, I was much older than both of them. I was forty-one and Madam was

24

twenty-four. She was expecting the twins. Ssebo was twenty-nine. Madam was tiny and her belly looked too big, as if its weight would upset her balance and make her fall on her back. But no, she was strong, and she would manage. I knew she carried twins even before she told me.

Later, I learnt to do things the way she wanted. I also learnt to tell when she was not happy. She would say, "Ok, Robinah, it will do," and I would know that she wanted it differently but she realized that the old dog's ability to learn new tricks was average at best.

I always wished she would allow herself a little trip into the past. Just a sneak peek would have done her no harm.

One time when the twins were eight and Pamela was seven . . . yes, that was the holiday when Cindy came to stay with them. Madam had come back around midnight from a celebration held in her honour. Ssebo was away on one of his business trips. I had not yet slept; I didn't go to bed before she came home, especially when Ssebo was away. I stood outside, waiting to help her just in case she had anything for me to carry inside. I opened the door as she drove her Range Rover into the garage. I stood outside and waited.

The lights of the houses on Muyenga Hill blinked in the late night. The sky was a clear dark blue and there were just a few stars visible. It had been a hot day but the night was refreshingly cool with a breeze from Lake Victoria. Madam emerged from the garage and stared at the sky for some seconds, before greeting me and handing me her file holder. She no longer had time to sit outside and gaze at the night sky, which she used to enjoy doing before the birth of her children. Her preoccupation with her work at Hope for Street Children now took precedence.

25

Mrs. Vanita Konko, known as Vicky to her friends but Madam to me, passed through the front door, and I followed. She looked elegant in her business suit as she entered her home that evening. It was quiet. The children were asleep. She did not go up to her room as I thought she would.

She sat in the black leather chair and placed the yellow and red cushions behind her back for comfort. She asked me if I thought the children were fast asleep. I told her they had slept early and so must be deep asleep. She thought for a moment, then went upstairs and opened the boys' room. The nine-year-old twins, Hans and Hedrick, were sprawled in their beds. She called out their names but they did not stir. She moved on to her daughter's room; seven-year-old Pamela was also fast asleep. She shared the room with her cousin Cindy, who had come to spend the holidays. She was three years older than Pamela but they got on well. Madam called out her name, too, but got no answer.

I turned away so I would not look her in the face. She had returned late from work the previous night, and had left early this morning, and now she had met the children asleep again. Ssebo was worse because he was forever on the move. It was like that every day, and it was likely to get worse, especially as Madam was taking on more responsibilities at the office. I had heard her explain their kind of life, when talking with friends who visited on Sundays: "I have to work, otherwise how will I provide for them? They have to go to good universities abroad. The ones here are terrible. Even for secondary schools, I will take them out."

"You are right, Vicky. Joe and I have thought about it and we are hoping to do the same," said Anita Mulu, one of her good friends. Anita and her husband were in the supermarket retail business.

26

That night when she looked into the children's rooms, all those explanations and plans seemed to melt away. Although I could see that she was tired, she did not seem to be in a hurry to go to bed. My guess was that after celebrating her promotion with outsiders, she was hoping it would be followed by a family celebration. Just then, as I watched her from the corner of my eye and wished I could say something to make her feel better, she decided to have a glass of wine.

"Robinah, please get me some wine," she said.

"OK, Madam."

"Red wine please. They say it is good for the heart."

I went to the liquor cabinet of polished wood. I picked a bottle of red wine and placed it on the table in front of Madam.

"Thank you," she told me, "you do not have to wait for me. Just check that the door is properly locked and then you can go to sleep. Our donors are visiting the office tomorrow. I will need to leave early."

"OK, Madam. Have a good night," I answered. I assumed she wanted to have time alone to think about her role as the new CEO of Hope for Street Children.

She poured herself a glass of the Italian red wine and settled deeper into the couch. Franklin Konko, her husband, was not expected back from one of his trips for another two weeks. He had not attended her promotion celebration, but she could not complain. I had heard them many times when they discussed these issues; they agreed that work was always first and foremost. That was why they were able to own a five-bedroom two-storey house with a private gym and swimming pool in this suburb of Kampala.

27

By 6 a.m. the next morning, Madam was ready for breakfast. She was a meticulous woman; she always left home at about 6.45 a.m. in order to beat the traffic across the city. The word "late" was not in her vocabulary.

This was during the school holidays. The children did not have to wake up early. That day, they did not wake up until after 8 a.m., and by then their mother was gone. It was Hedrick, the younger twin, who woke up first. He rushed to his parents' bedroom. "Mummy!" he yelled as he opened the door. There was no answer. The room was empty. He stood in the doorway. The double bed was made, so it looked as if it had not been slept in. "Mummy!" he called again. Then he entered and closed the door behind him.

A few minutes later, Hans entered the room. He too called for his mother as he opened the door. His words bounced off the walls. Empty silence greeted him. It was then that he saw his brother lying on the big bed, eyes closed, his thumb in his mouth. He approached the bed and shook him. "Hedrick, wake up, let's go. I will tell Mummy you are sucking your thumb again."

Hedrick opened his eyes. "Where is she?" he asked.

"I will tell her when she comes," Hans answered.

I stood at the bottom of the stairs and listened to their exchange. If only Madam knew how much her children missed her, I thought to myself. Then I called out to them: "Hedrick, Hans, come down for breakfast. I can hear you talking. Hurry up . . . and call Pamela and Cindy too."

"Hedrick, Robinah is calling us, let's go," Hans told his brother.

In a short while, they were downstairs in the kitchen.

When Madam and Ssebo were not around, which was the case most of the time, the children had their meals with me in the kitchen.

Pamela did not come down. While the boys ate, I walked upstairs to call her and Cindy. They were awake. "Why have you not come to have your breakfast?" I need not have asked. Pamela was sitting on the carpet with a colouring book and paint brushes. She liked painting and colouring and she was always bent over these books. At seven years old, she painted well, but today she was in a mood for experimentation: the faces of the people were green, the plants were red and the dog was purple.

"What are you painting?" I asked her.

"Take a look." She held out the book to me.

"Pam, people are not green. And have you ever seen a purple dog?"

"This holiday, I will be using only my favourite colours. You see all these books—" she said, pointing to the stack of colouring books her father had brought her from South Africa, "I will be using only these colours. They are my favourite colours. They're the only ones I want to see." She said this with a smile of satisfaction as she turned the pages for me to see. Well, as Madam always said, I lived in a different world. So I could not understand Pamela, who found her own way to cope by painting only in her favourite colours.

My journey into the past comes to a stop as I notice that everyone has stood up and they are singing. I stand up too and join in the singing of the Luganda song *Yesu Obw'alikomawo*, When Jesus Comes Back. Imagine, Hedrick, Madam and Ssebo and the rest

29

of the family singing about Jesus' return! And who chose the songs to be sung for Hedrick at his last rites? He or she should have known that Hedrick would never forgive that person for localizing him, yes, even in death! He never spoke a word of any of the native languages, and neither did any of his siblings. I remembered that many times I would speak to the children and they would just look at me as if I were carrying a monkey on my back!

One time, before Hans and Hedrick went to South Africa for secondary school, the late Samuel Bagi, father of Ssebo, came to visit his grandchildren. He had been a minister in one of the past governments, but by the time of his visit he was already retired from active service.

He summoned Ssebo the day after he arrived. Konko was the name he liked to call him, because that was the name he had given him, and it was also the name of his own grandfather. It was Sunday morning and they sat beside each other on the spacious balcony overlooking Lake Victoria. I served them beers and the other worker, Jingo, was roasting goat meat for them.

"I want to take Hans, Hedrick and Pamela home with me when I leave on Tuesday," Samuel Bagi said.

"Hmm. That would be good but . . ."

"But what?"

"Well, as I said, it would be good. But sincerely, *Mzee*, it is a little abrupt."

"Abrupt? How do you want me to do it? Do I need to write a proposal and then wait for an answer in six weeks? Is that what you want me to do?"

"*Mzee*, you know I do not mean it that way."

"Alright, listen to me then. You see, these children are leaving home at a tender age. The boys are just thirteen, and I know that next year Pamela will also join them. Is that not so?"

"Yes, she will, because that is the only way to give them the best education."

"I understand. But if it were me, I would let them attend secondary school here, and then go far away for university."

"*Mzee*, we have been through all of this already."

"I am saying it for emphasis. I know you will not take my advice, but just remember it anyway. Please, let me take these children with me, so that they will get a feel of where they come from."

"But they have been there before. *Mzee*, you know they have been there."

"Yes, I do, but you always stay for only two or three days. And you people have not been there in the last one and a half years. Now, when I go with them, without you, they will be relaxed and I will have time to tell them stories like I used to tell you. Have you ever told them those stories?"

"No, but I will. I am going to make a point of doing so. But *Mzee*, things are not the same as they were during the time when I was growing up. Today, I hardly have any time to spare."

"I understand my son. And that is why I want to help. If I take them with me, they will learn a lot. By the time they return, they will truly know who they are, and you and your wife will be pleasantly surprised."

"I understand, but we had already made different plans. We want to spend some time in Nairobi, and then go on

31

to South Africa to do our shopping, all in one month. So, *Mzee*, it is not possible now, but we shall do it when they come back for their first holiday. I promise."

Mzee made a sound. It was not laughter; it was more of a snort, as if he wanted to laugh but choked on something.

"Do not take these things for granted, Konko. But thanks anyway for considering it."

By the time the boys came for the holidays, *Mzee's* health was not good, and he died soon after. I do not know whether Ssebo ever remembered this conversation with his father.

#

They were making speeches now. The congregation was attentive and many people were sniffing and drying tears. There was a group of Hedrick's friends, about ten of them. Three were lined up to speak. Hedrick had grown to be a warm and friendly person: I was not surprised that such a large crowd turned up for his funeral. Some friends had even come all the way from South Africa, where he had opted to remain for university after he graduated from secondary school. He was supposed to have been completing his degree in Architecture but it was discovered that he had attended only the first year of his course before dropping out of school. But nobody knew of this until his parents became suspicious a few years later and crosschecked with the university.

I remember the time Madam and Ssebo travelled together to South Africa and came back with Hedrick. The mood around the house was sombre, as if someone had died. It was like the black spot on the skin of a mango that tells you a worm has found its way inside and you are likely to find only rotted flesh. That was nearly two years ago, and the rot had spread, eating up Hedrick's twenty-two-year-old body. Here he was now, stretched out on a church podium, dead.

Madam and Ssebo would talk late into the night and at times they would be with other people. There were two people who came regularly. I got to know that one was a doctor and the other a counsellor. At times, Hedrick would sit with them. That was when I found out.

#

Hedrick's friends were still delivering speeches. They looked smart today in their black suits. I knew a number of them. Many times I had cooked for them when they came to visit Hedrick. I could see the shock on their faces. Almost always they would cry; for Hedrick, but also for themselves, because they knew that it could have easily been any of them in his place.

After he came back from South Africa, his parents begged him to show them that he had changed. He tried, but some of the habits he had picked up would not let him stay changed for long.

#

The friends had finished speaking; many heads were bent, crying into their handkerchiefs. The service was over. It was time to go. The Funeral Services staff carried out the casket. They marched out of the church. Madam was supported by a friend. Cindy's arm was around Pamela's shoulders. Ssebo walked next to them, looking haggard. The four days since the death of his son had aged him, sapped his spirit. Hans stared straight ahead like a man who had lost his sight. His uncle, Ssebo's brother, put his arm around the waist of Hedrick's twin as they shuffled behind the casket.

33

There was the customary viewing of the body. I did not want to see the body. I did not want to see his face, dark, lifeless, and twisted with pain. My Hedrick! No, no, no! I wanted to keep the mind image of him as I remembered him best. As he took his first faltering steps and I, arms stretched, waited to catch him if he fell. I remembered the infant laughter as I fed him and his brother.

The Funeral Service staff lifted the casket into their shiny black van. We were to start the journey to the village to place him in his "final resting place". That was what the master of ceremony had called it. I knew this place. The picture was so clear in my mind. I had been there to bury his grandfather. It was a corner in the neat compound below Samuel Bagi's house. Hedrick would be laid next to him. The two of them, old man and young man, would have time together at last to talk late into the night through the walls of their separate chambers. I could hear their conversation.

"You have come too early, Hedrick . . . what brought you here?"

"You see, Grandpa, it was just a harmless pastime, just a type of cigarette, different, you know what I mean, Grandpa. Just because . . . oh . . ."

"I did not hear you, my son. Will you speak louder?"

"I said, just because I made a mistake . . . and overdosed . . . oh, it was so bad!"

Then all is silent.

#

The funeral procession is now moving, snaking through the bustling city streets. We will reach Buwamba in the early evening, Hedrick's final resting place.

34

Burial Rites for Tisa

Mary Mzyece Sililo

Sunga woke up to the sound of loud wailing. She listened again and in her sleepy state, it was like somebody was reciting some eerie poetry. She concluded that her nieces were listening to a late radio programme. She swung both feet from the bed with the intention of storming into the room of whoever was causing the racket. What met her eyes when she opened the door put a stop to all her intentions.

Her seventy-five-year-old mother was parading the small corridor, a *chitenje* wrapped around her waist. Her wrinkled belly fell over her *chitenje* cloth in one flap. She was beating her chest while wailing and imploring the ancestors to have mercy on her. She would stop once in a while to cup her sagging breasts and rock them up and down as if comforting them. Not that there was much to rock; those breasts looked like old dry ropes made from the bark of a tree. Breastfeeding thirteen children had taken its toll on her body.

The truth hit Sunga like a slap in the face. Her sister, who had been ill for the past five years, had died. Sunga felt sorry for her mother. No amount of preparation, mental or otherwise, could have readied her for the pain she was now feeling. She had given birth to thirteen children, raised and educated them singlehandedly by sheer hard work and determination. Having been the first of three wives, she was neglected by her husband, who dutifully turned up at her hut only to impregnate her and then move on to his favourite wife, a girl who was the same age as his daughters.

Sunga's father and his other two wives were early victims of HIV/AIDS. Enala, Sunga's mother, had miraculously escaped the scourge. This had not endeared her to her in-laws, who had accused her of bewitching her husband and his wives. Enala had to leave the village and take refuge with her widowed eldest daughter, Brenda.

The AIDS pandemic visited Enala's family in full force and she started burying her children one after the other. Sunga remembered how in one year they had buried three of her siblings, including Brenda, leaving Enala destitute. It was inevitable that she had to move in with Sunga. Within three years, Enala was left with only four children. Sunga, who was the sixth-born, was now the eldest child alive. She had never married, preferring to be a single parent to four of her dead siblings' children.

Tisa, the sister who followed Sunga, had been a doctor and had moved to the UK with her youngest son after her divorce. At the beginning of Tisa's illness, it was decided she should come back to Zambia to be nursed by her mother and sister. Tisa's son had not liked the idea. He argued that the UK had better medical facilities and whoever wanted to help nurse his mother should find a way of getting there. Sunga could not do so because of her commitments, and Enala was afraid of flying.

36

Zondo, Sunga's only living brother, who worked in Botswana, paid Tisa a visit and stayed with her for three months. He brought back news that Tisa had only a few months to live. The news broke their mother's heart even though she put up a brave face for her children's sake.

Being a small woman, Enala presented a deceptive picture of her personality. She had a gentle face that gave the impression that she was not sure of herself and needed protection and guidance. Her relatives were shocked at her insistence that Tisa's body be brought back so that she could be buried in the land of her ancestors. Sunga dutifully relayed the information to Tisa's son in the UK.

"That's impossible, Aunty. It would be too costly and in any case, I wouldn't be able to attend the funeral as I'm in the UK illegally."

That was news to Sunga. "What do you mean, John? I personally helped your mother to get a student's visa for you ..."

"Yes, Aunty, but that was years ago. I completed my studies and just stayed on. I'm now working illegally." John said this with finality. Sunga could not argue any more. "Why can't Granny come here? At least she ..."

"Forget it. Mother can't see herself in those metallic birds. I tried to put her in one to go for her sister's funeral in the village; the whole thing was an embarrassment. In any case, mother is adamant that Tisa's body should be brought back here to appease the ancestors otherwise they will start taking even her grandchildren."

"Well, I have another suggestion that will solve both my problems and Granny's."

37

"What is it?"

"We cremate the body here."

"We do what?"

"Yes Aunty. That way, I will attend the cremation ceremony here and then Granny will have the remains of her daughter in form of ashes." Sunga was shocked by this suggestion. The only words that formed on her tongue were, *How cruel!* but she did not voice them.

"You see, ashes will be cheaper to transport. I can easily give them to any of my friends travelling . . ." John continued.

Sunga took a deep breath, and weighed the options. Cremation was not part of their cultural practices. Yet, she had to admit, it seemed the most practical.

"Hello Aunty . . . are you still there?" John's voice brought her back to reality.

"Yes, I am."

"Aha?"

"I am listening."

"Did you hear me? I was saying . . ."

"I heard you."

"And?"

"Ah . . . I'll tell mother. I will tell her and hear what she has to say," Sunga answered, her voice almost inaudible even to herself.

#

Enala would not hear of it. She did not understand how her grandson would even think of making a *braai* out of her daughter. She gave an impromptu recital of what seemed like poetry.

Now they want to make burnt meat out of you
You who deserves the death of a cow at your funeral

38

You who should be buried on a cow's hide
And the meat roasted instead of you
If only I could see the soil you will lie on
The soil that is not your ancestors'
The soil that will cradle you the way I used to . . .

Enala went on and on, about not throwing soil onto the grave that her precious daughter would be buried in, and not being able to lie on the mound of soil under which her Tisa would spend eternity. The women who sat with her joined their wails to hers. And up in smoke went the cremation idea.

Sunga racked her brain to think of something that would be acceptable to both sides. John was getting impatient and threatening to bury his mother with or without his grandmother's input. "In any case, it is very expensive to keep a body in the morgue here," he complained when Sunga reported Enala's reaction to the idea of cremation.

Enala's recitations gave Sunga an idea. She invited two elderly relatives to discuss it. They all agreed it was a better alternative, and one Enala would appreciate under the circumstances. Three female relatives were selected to go and talk to her and explain that it would be almost impossible to transport the body from the UK, but that it would be possible to get some of the soil Tisa was going to lie in. Enala cried but the trio noted that her cries were of resigned acceptance. The women sighed with relief at finding an acceptable solution to the dilemma. Sunga on the other hand wondered how the plan would be executed as she went to call Tisa's son.

John laughed at the idea. "And who do you think will get into a plane with a packet of soil?" he mocked. "Come on, Aunty . . . what does the person say to the security men at the airport? It's easy to explain ashes, but soil? They might take him for a terrorist. He might have to miss his flight while they take the soil for testing. In any case, no one would agree to such an absurd idea. I would not find anybody to bring the soil home."

Sunga was disappointed by the ridicule in John's voice, yet she remained hopeful that the soil could be sent.

#

That is how Sunga found herself on an international flight for the first time. She was on her way to the UK to attend the funeral of her sister, Tisa. She took along some Zambian soil taken from the Leopards' Hill Cemetery where two of her siblings were buried. Her mother, Enala, had insisted on it. Enala had scooped the soil with her bare hands and said some farewell words as she poured it into a plastic bag. It had been well wrapped, and it was packed away in a suitcase that Sunga checked in.

John met her at Heathrow Airport. Contrary to what he had said, she passed through airport security without incident. Her small parcel did not attract any attention. "You were just lucky," John said.

At the cemetery, when she got out the soil from Zambia to throw onto the grave, a few curious eyes looked at her and she felt as if she was performing some incomprehensible African ritual among unfriendly strangers. The harder part, however, was taking the soil from the grave. Sunga and her nephew had to wait until everyone had left. Then they knelt down by the grave as if in prayer, gathered some soil and put it in a plastic bag.

That done, she turned her attention to the next task she had to perform. Enala had given her strict instructions to go through the deceased's personal belongings and bring back everything that was personal and intimate. It was a lonely affair. She could not ask her nephew to help. A son is not allowed to handle his mother's underwear.

Sunga got the clothes out of the wardrobe and sorted them into two heaps. One heap was to be discarded in the UK, while the other heap would be taken back to Zambia and shared out among relatives in the village. Then she rummaged through the drawers. Her sister had always been a neat girl. Sunga smiled at the memory of the fights they had had as children over Tisa's suitcase. Tisa always knew if anybody had tampered with her belongings. Pulling out the first drawer, Sunga noticed the panties neatly stacked in the left hand corner and the bras on the right. Sunga took out all of these and packed them in a plastic bag, which she put in the suitcase. These were not to be shared out for fear of witchcraft. She turned back to check that she had removed all the underwear from the drawer. In the far corner, she found a rubber object. It was shaped like something familiar. Her eyes widened. She could not believe what she held in her hand.

She had heard that women in the western world bought these shapes to gratify their sexual desires, but she could not believe that her sister had needed the services of a plastic thing. "Maybe white men here did not propose love to black women?" She could not believe that either, because back home, white men chased black girls as much as black men did. "Could it be that the cold weather dampened their sexual desires?" She dismissed that as well, because books had taught her that men would always be men, anywhere.

She examined the object in her hands and noticed that it worked with batteries. She laughed at the thought of somebody using such an unnatural method. She remembered

41

how particular her sister had been about health issues: she had left her husband because he refused to use a condom in spite of his promiscuity. "There must be a shortage of men in the UK," Sunga concluded loudly. She was leaving the following day, so she hastily packed her things and returned the banana-shaped plastic thing to its dark corner.

John hurried her up the following morning. It was then that Sunga realized she could not leave the thing for her nephew to look at. It was taboo for children to even imagine their mother's sexuality. She opened the drawer, drew it out, and flung it into her handbag.

Sunga felt confident as she went through the airport clearance. She had nothing of value or anything suspicious-looking. So it came as a surprise when the woman at the security desk started rummaging through her hand language and pulled out the bag of soil and the plastic thing.

"What's this?" the security woman asked sternly, peering at the sensual object.

Sunga pursed her lips, which gave her face an uncompromising expression. She dwarfed the lady; Sunga was a tall woman.

"What does it look like?" she retorted.

The woman glared back, awaiting an explanation.

"I need it as a teaching aid when showing children how to wear condoms." She silently thanked God for the lessons she gave as a social worker to some boys who came to the welfare centre that she ran back home. The stern-faced woman was taken aback, but her training would not allow her to give up the questioning.

"And what about this?"

"It is soil from my sister's grave that I am taking back home for burial rites."

At these words, the security woman looked at her as if she has just landed from Mars, then she waved her on.

#

The flight back to her home was uneventful. Sunga's younger brother, Zondo, was at the airport to meet her. He confirmed that everything was ready for Tisa's funeral in the village the following day.

"The cow we will slaughter has already been selected and people have gathered at the home of our uncle. I'm sure we will be through in one day and back in town by the third day."

Sunga was amazed at how much effort her mother had put into Tisa's traditional burial. Sunga wondered what her relatives would think of the materials that she brought back.

"With all her things that I have brought back from the UK, I'm sure our sister's funeral will be handled to the satisfaction of our mother and our ancestral spirits," Sunga said. "How is mother?"

"She is fine. She is the only one at home right now. The rest have already left for the village to prepare for the burial. The three of us shall leave first thing tomorrow."

Sunga was grateful for that. She had dreaded the thought of finding the house full of mourners. It was important that her mother got the privilege of looking through her late daughter's things in private. That way, Enala could sort things out and have enough time to come to terms with whatever had happened to Tisa.

Enala cried when she saw Sunga; the two of them hugged and comforted each other. After Sunga had rested, Enala entered her room and asked her about the trip. They talked about John and wondered if he would ever return. Then Sunga showed her the soil and Enala cried over it as she held it to her breast. She surprised Sunga by asking her if Tisa had married.

"But Mother, you know she was a divorcée."

"Yes, but she was too young to have been without a man in her life . . . and I knew my daughter, she was not like you."

"Mother!" Sunga exclaimed, but Enala was undaunted. "A foreign man will never ask us to cleanse him. He will be going around with Tisa's spirit."

Sunga took that as the cue to show her mother the thing that she had brought back. She pulled her bag close and pulled it out. Her mother looked at it in bewilderment. From the look on her face, Sunga could tell her mother recognized the shape.

"This is what Tisa was using, Mother." Enala stared at her daughter in disbelief. "It uses batteries." Sunga turned it to show where the batteries would go. As comprehension sank in, Enala's eyes looked as if they would pop out of their sockets.

"No wonder she got ill. This thing can kill any woman," she said at last.

"No, Mother, this can't make anybody ill. Tisa had cancer of the liver; this would never kill anybody."

"But how are we going to cleanse it?" Sunga had hoped that the cleansing issue would be forgotten. "If we don't, Tisa's spirit will never rest. Had it been a man of flesh and blood, it would have been easy. A medicine man would have found a way of making Sunga's spirit rest even if the man was not available. But this . . ." She looked perplexed. Sunga felt sorry for her.

"Well, Mother, sexual cleansing is not practised anymore due to HIV/AIDS. All we have to do is show the relatives Tisa's things and they will perform the burial rites. That will take care of that."

"I can't do that with this. Other items, yes, but not this," Enala said, grabbing the thing and putting it behind her. "I can't allow the villagers to look at this and make fun of my daughter."

"But mother, I thought you wanted her spirit to rest . . ."

"Yes I do." She stared at Sunga intently. "You said this wouldn't make anybody ill . . . that it can't kill anybody?" Tisa nodded. "You, her sister, shall keep her secret," she continued almost feverishly. "You'll know what to do with this." Looking into her eyes, she placed the object in Sunga's hands.

Sunga did not ask her mother what she wanted her to do with the vibrator. She could see it in her unblinking eyes.

LeavingOxfordStreet

Molara Wood

*S*he asks if I will come with her to Oxford. "Oxford Street, you mean." I laugh into the phone receiver. "How many times do I have to tell you, Yeni? Oxford Street. Get it right, will you?"

"Will you come?" It's like she hasn't heard me. Yeni has been in London eight months. As is typical of some newly arrived Nigerians, she calls the famous street "Oxford".

"I could use the company," she says. I suddenly regret telling her I am free for the day. Not sure I want to tag along for another round of compulsive spending.

"We can also drop by to see Maryam," she adds. "What do you say?"

Maryam swings it. I arrive at Yeni's house in Kingsbury within the hour. Her husband Dayo is pottering about upstairs. He doesn't call down a "hello" but he makes enough noise for me to know he is home. Dayo da Costa, inveterate snob. How Yeni ended up with him I don't know, but the financial security must compensate, I think, as I sink into the endless softness of the beige leather suite.

I hazard an easy guess. "Are we going to Selfridges by any chance?"

"I have to pick up some stuff there." Yeni pats her belly. Seven months gone. Every other day there's something new she has to pick up for the baby.

"Your favourite place in London," I once teased her. "I bet you'll go into labour in there one of these days. We'll name the baby Miss Selfridge!"

"Who says it's going to be a girl?" she had replied.

Yeni wants a boy, a British-born boy who would be able to travel the world as a subject of the Crown. Who would not need a visa to hop on the Eurostar to Paris or jump on a plane for a short trip to Atlanta. We told her she is some decades late. Margaret Thatcher took care of generations of our yet unborn on these isles long ago. Since 1981, children born in Britain to foreigners no longer have an automatic right to citizenship — surely Yeni knew that? Whether it is the former British Premier or the hormones, Yeni is always grumpy. One time when we heard on the news that someone had decapitated a statue of Thatcher, Yeni laughed and laughed.

"I can at least have a boy, even if he can't be a citizen — yet. Damn that Thatcher woman," she moaned on another occasion.

I couldn't resist stating the obvious. "You really have taken this citizenship snub as a personal insult."

"With the indignity awaiting every green-passport-carrying Nigerian in the airports and consulates of the Western world, can you blame me?" She leaned forward and put her hands on her hips. "Your friend who went to America, what's her name — why do you think she left this country clutching a Russian passport?"

48

"Don't bring Ronke into this," I said. "You hardly knew her.... I really don't think it's the same situation. There is a whole history to Ronke's dual nationality."

"History or no history, she is not going to be throwing away that passport soon now, is she?"

"Anyway," I said with a wave of the hand, "Ronke knows as well as anyone that a European passport is not the solution to everything."

"Easy for you to say, Folake, you with your UK Right of Abode!"

That shut me up.

#

Yeni struggles with a pair of flat-heeled boots trimmed with faux fur. She can't bend forward because of the bump, so she shuffles sideways in an ungainly fashion, one hand on the dining table for support. She breathes heavily. Boots on, she waddles away to get her coat.

"Someone said I could go and have the baby in America," she says in a raised voice from the hallway, returning to her favourite topic. "The Americans still have an old-fashioned decency about babies born on their soil apparently, bless them. But Dayo won't hear of it."

Dayo tires of pottering about and heads downstairs, his footfalls taking affected pauses on the hardwood steps of the stairway.

"The lengths our people go to," he says with a snort, "to have future Nigerians with European and American passports!" His texturised, short-cropped hair has a middle parting in front. His accent has begun to ape the plummy tones of the landed gentry. Dayo is one of those Lagos old-money types who no

49

longer have it, but like to behave as though they never lost their glory. A descendant of Brazilian returnees, he was not expected to marry Yeni, the daughter of a Yoruba trader-made-good from Osogbo whom he met at the Nigerian Law School. He relocated to London to take her away from the derision of his family, who believe he married beneath him. Now he never seems to let Yeni forget the fact. I thought she had humanised him, but now I am not so sure. A job as the only black in a posh city law firm has brought out the uppity in Dayo. He pretends the citizenship thing is ridiculous but his laughter rings hollow enough for me to know that deep inside he would have been glad for it.

"Hi," I say to him. One must tolerate one's friend's husband, however unpleasant the man.

"Hello, Folake," he replies, but neglects to look my way. He passes through the dining area, his back to me, headed towards the kitchen. Yeni re-enters from the hallway, coat on, and moves quickly to stand in his path. Never one to shy away from confrontation.

"Maybe your parents will respect me more if I brought them a British citizen for a grandchild, what do you think?"

He steps around her and waves a dismissive hand. "Have fun spending my money out there today, darling," he says over his shoulder.

#

Japanese tourists smile at us outside Bond Street Station. The lead man asks for the way to Selfridges. He doesn't say it quite right, but we know where he means to go. I point the way, and they are soon lost in the throngs of shoppers. We follow in the same direction, inching along in an unhurried procession of shuffling feet.

50

"You will really love this place come Christmastime," I tell Yeni. "Everything lit and twinkling, quite a sight. One Christmas, there were 260 thousand light bulbs on this street alone."

"Wow, Folake. And there I was thinking you didn't like me dragging you out here!"

"Oh well."

"Will you miss London when you go back home?" Yeni asks as we reach a set of traffic lights. A bicycle whizzes past and I step back. The cross-flow of people edges me further out. A steady stream of shoppers now flows between me and Yeni, and with others milling behind, I am walled in by people. Yeni remains beside the traffic light pole, peering over the heads at me, amused at my crowd complication. I smile back. At least this way I don't have to engage with her question. Not another inquisition about why I want to be called to the English Bar rather than attend Law School in Nigeria after I graduate in a few months' time. Not another frown as she wonders what my parents make of my plans. She always asks this, though I've explained time and again that Dad is fine with it, or at least doesn't protest. And even Mum's given up now. "Nigeria has a way of reclaiming her own, eventually," Mum had said; and I guess I can live with that, whatever it means.

A gap opens in the stream and I step up beside Yeni. She's forgotten her question, and I'm relieved. Or it might have ended as usual, with her getting all righteous about my wanting to stay in this country while I preach about her desire for a British baby. It's not the same thing, I always tell her. How is it different, she demands. I refrain from saying mine is a mere preference; I am not running from hostile, high-minded in-laws like she is.

51

Five double-decker buses are backed up one after another in the traffic, forming a wall of red in the street. Green lights turn to red, but the wall remains. We run out of patience and trail other feet through the gash between two buses. By the time we arrive under the clock above Selfridges' main entrance, Yeni's talk is only of things to buy. The store is teeming with people and their voices hum. Yeni picks up a trial tub of Visible Difference on the Elizabeth Arden counter and tests the cream, middle finger of one hand moisturising the back of the other in rotating motions.

"It's very popular with Nigerian women, you know," I tell her. "Maryam told me that many Lagos ladies visiting London rush to the nearest Arden stockists to ask for — wait for it — 'Invisible Difference'."

"Invisible Difference!" Yeni gives a loud cackle at the misnomer. She places the tub back in its moulded space on the display. "When is the best time to catch Maryam, by the way?"

"She goes to lunch at one. We can make it if we hurry."

We join women of colour milling around the Fashion Fair stand. One assistant is seeing to a customer who tries a concealer for the blotches on her bleached skin. "Is it for yellow people?" the customer asks the Fashion Fair lady in a West African accent whose specific source I can't place. Yeni's eyes widen on hearing the black woman classify herself as "yellow" on account of a complexion that came out of the bottle. I pull her away before the hormones can speak, and we go seeking the baby department. Romper suits in 'boy colours', a shawl and two pairs of booties in the Selfridges' yellow carrier-bag later, we head for the store where Maryam works. Her supervisor, who's now used to us, smiles and tells our friend to clock off five minutes early.

"So what's this I hear about our women misjiving and asking for Invisible Difference?" Yeni asks Maryam as we sit down for tea and coffee in a St. Christopher's Place café. She chuckles in anticipation of a reply, but Maryam only gives a thin smile. I give Maryam a long look. Black Senegalese twists coifed on her head give a look of modern African royalty and accentuate the nut-brown sheen of her skin. We've discovered to our surprise that cheekbones are desirable in the West, and Maryam's are outstanding. Customers walk slowly past her counter just to give her a closer look. They might look at her differently if they knew she no longer has a valid visa.

"What is it, Maryam?" I ask.

"Oh, it's just this job, you know." She is yet to touch her chocolate muffin or coffee, and is instead tracing the arch of one eyebrow with a French manicured finger.

Maryam's job complements her model-like mien. Glamorous, and the pay isn't bad. We know people with worse jobs. *Gburu*, we call those jobs. Roughing it to scrape a living.

I smile. "But you love your job."

"Not when I get the kind of customer I had today."

"So, what happened with this customer?" Yeni wipes pastry crusts from her mouth and leaves a bold lipstick-smudge on her napkin.

Maryam sighs. "Customers are like cosmetics, I guess. All sorts."

"Get to it. What's the story? We're listening."

I chide Yeni with a pinch under the table. She glares at me. Maryam doesn't notice and launches into her story. She tested foundations on the back of a customer's hand to help select the

53

right consistency and shade. The customer, an English lady, chose an oil-free liquid one in Soft Peach. Maryam then dabbed cleansing lotion on cotton wool and wiped the customer's hand. The white lady looked at the black girl cleaning her hand and shook her head. "You people have no shame," she had said, looking right into Maryam's eyes.

"What did she mean, *you people*?" Maryam asks, slapping both hands on the table. Her cup rattles and dark liquid trickles down the side onto the saucer. "Because I was doing my job by tending to her, does that mean I'm slavish, that I have no pride? And what's it got to do with my people?"

"No point asking us now," Yeni retorts with a hard stare. "You should have asked the idiot of a woman what she meant right there and then."

"You are being a bit unfair, Yeni," I say. "You can hardly expect Maryam to get into a situation with a customer, especially in that kind of environment."

"Folake, don't give me any of that 'customer is always right' crap. If someone tells me to my face that I and my people have no shame, I will give her a lesson she'll never forget!"

Yeni pours herself more tea and signals the waitress for extra milk. She doesn't have to earn a living and so cannot understand why someone like Maryam has to keep her head down at work, especially with a precarious immigration status.

"Try not to think about it." I pat Maryam's hand. She nods, eyes lowered, wearing her glamour like a wretched sack. In the glass window of the tiny jewellery shop next door, fossilised insects float in crafted amber, suspended in a warm resinous glow.

#

"Me, I would never stand for it, not from anybody," Yeni is saying as we go down the escalator into the underground station. Maryam is back at her counter, and we are leaving Oxford Street. We arrive on the platform as the train pulls in. We are ahead of the rush hour and the carriage is half empty; no need to hope someone will give up a seat for a pregnant woman.

Five youths board the train several stations later and increase the number of black passengers in the carriage to seven. They chase themselves noisily up and down the carriage, not minding who they step on. Yeni looks at me and shakes her head. With my eyes, I plead with her to say nothing. Two of the boys start to swing from the train's handlebars while the others continue to barge about. Passengers pretend not to notice, each looking into an undefined space in front of their noses, staring into nothing. The gang turn their attention to a young man at the other end of the carriage, and there is cackling laughter as they taunt him, prodding him. Yeni throws me an anxious look, torn between saying something and acting like the other passengers, who keep straight faces. How very England, I think, and how one is compelled to behave in the same way.

The youths part the young man from his rucksack and play catch with it. They act with impunity till the train pulls into the next stop where they jump off, laughing like this is the biggest joke ever. Then, as if bored with their own antics, they throw the rucksack back onto the train as the doors begin to bleep to indicate they will soon shut. Sandy hair flops onto the young man's forehead, partially obscuring his face as he bends down to pick the rucksack from the train floor. He dabs at his eyes with his jacket sleeve.

"Bastards! How dare you treat him like that?" Yeni's voice thumps the air like a fog-horn. Through the train's glass windows, I can see the boys' faces freeze. They have stopped laughing. One boy's trainer shoe is now wedged between the closing doors. He pries them forcefully apart and they yield, bleeping as they open wide. He comes back on board. I stiffen as Yeni grips me with both hands. We are in more trouble than the blond victim ever was. The gang leader towers over us and we cower in our seats. He brandishes an empty bottle. Spit rains with obscenities down onto our heads. Vile intents mask his hooded face as he bends closer. He has a plastic container of milkshake in the other hand and takes a swig between his ranting, as if gulping liquor for boldness.

No one moves. The passengers opposite us do not so much as look our way; the erstwhile victim minds his own business on the other side. Our tormentor raises the bottle. We are going to be punished for not minding our business. We are going to be scarred for life, or worse, for not acting like the others on this train. Then there is shouting from the platform, the rest of the gang warning that the train driver has become suspicious. I look from the platform to the ringleader's face and see that committing a serious assault has suddenly become dicey for him. He stuffs the bottle into his puffy jacket and turns to make a getaway. Then he looks back, from me to Yeni who, it now dawns on me, had managed to get a few words in edgeways through his invectives. He raises his other hand and brings it down in one swift movement. Thick, strawberry milkshake sails through the air, splattering in thick splodges down one side of Yeni's face and chest. She instinctively swipes with her hand so she can see through the one eye, but the mess only spreads. One side of her face seems melted into pink.

56

The moment occurs in slow time in my mind as the ringleader jumps, high and silent, onto the platform, a rogue stuntman. The train judders into life and soon we are in the tunnel. Yeni, hormonal and milkshake-faced, rises to her feet and fills the carriage with a booming noise.

"How could you just sit there and do nothing?" she yells at the other passengers. "Grown men like you! He could have hurt us seriously, that animal! How could you just sit there?" On and on she shouts.

"Well, you are all the same anyway," a man sitting cross-legged by the doors says with a shrug, finally. He looks resentful, that we have forced him out of his habitual reticence into speaking. He uncrosses his legs and his cheeks redden. I see his embarrassment, surprised at himself for voicing such a thing out loud.

At his words, Yeni gasps and places a hand on her belly. My hand has flown to cover my open mouth. This is what it comes down to: we and the dangerous youths disturbing the peace are one and the same. We are the same colour, after all. Yeni starts to rage again, screaming at the man, but he has resumed his cross-legged pose, pretending she is not there. In front of his averted face, his unruffled coolness, she looks deranged. I pull her off at the next stop.

"We said you could give birth to a Miss Selfridge," I attempt a joke as the train slides away from us, "not a Mister London Underground. It just doesn't have the same ring to it, you know?" Yeni smiles through her tears. She is in a heap on a platform bench, and I stand over her. I dig for tissues in my bag and clean her up and tidy her braids. We get on the next train. My mind bumps along with the shuddering train, too numb to think.

"Is this what we trouble so much for, Folake?" Yeni's voice reaches my ears. "To be seen as bad peas from the same black pod, same as those scumbags? Aren't those passengers scumbags themselves for not helping us just because we are the same colour as our attackers? And me, pregnant as I am?" She looks down at her belly. "Is this what I'm bringing my child into? What difference will it make if he is British?"

I say nothing. I know that if and when she gets over this, she will still want her child to be one thing, and that is British.

#

We are back at Yeni's place. Dayo says she had no business endangering herself and their unborn child by butting into a matter that didn't concern her. His face disappears behind *The Telegraph* as I get up to leave.

"Try not to think about that thing on the train," I tell Yeni at the door. I ask her to forget, for how else is she to have the baby she hopes will one day be British? I ask her to forget but I know I will not. Right there on her doorstep, I decide that I will go to law school in Nigeria after all. My mother will welcome that. "You were right," I will tell her, "Nigeria does have a way of reclaiming her own."

"Better we don't tell Maryam about the attack on the tube," Yeni says. "It would only compound her distress over that thing with the customer." The words tumble out of Yeni's mouth. The hands shake a little. Her unapologetic indignation has given way to a new timidity. Her fabulous bravado is gone.

"I almost forgot. That bloody customer!"

"Nothing's going to keep me from Oxford though," Yeni says, attempting a smile. "Oxford Street," she corrects herself.

"And if I'm free I'll come with you. Just let me know. Whenever."

"OK. Or maybe for a change we can go to Liverpool on a Sunday and check out the latest lace in the market. There's also that shop that sells fresh chicken that tastes just like back home."

Liverpool Street, she means to say.

A World of Our Own

Elizabeth Namakula Lenana

Uncle Kim Meyers looked out over Yokohama Bay. He wasn't my uncle. We called every adult on the team either Aunt or Uncle as a way of showing respect. There were ships in the bay, laden with cargo comprising of Japanese automobile parts, as we were later told. Other ships carried tourists, sightseeing.

Uncle Kim seemed uneasy, his brow knitted in thought. We loved him a lot. He was our team leader. He was white, an American, but that was the only difference between us. We were on a tour of Japan, telling our stories of war—as former child soldiers—and of the life we had found in Wakisa Children's Homes where we had gone after a brief stint at the rehabilitation camps in Pader.

Uncle Kim roused himself and called out to us. We all gathered around him. "Please take your positions," he said softly. We all loved being part of the choir. We were going to sing for the people on the top floor of the Pentagon Plaza, which overlooked the bay. We were all adorned in cream pants and black T-shirts with the words "Child Soldier No More."

61

Aunt Rose, our choir conductor, stood in front of us as we giggled and took positions. She motioned to us to look at her. As usual she made funny faces, and we laughed. She always did this to make us relax on stage. When we started singing, our voices were low at first. Then we sang louder, looking at Aunt Rose for instructions in her arms and her face. We had the attention of everyone in the lobby. We sang a cappella versions of two songs. We could tell that the songs touched the audience by the way they moved their eyes and heads, with interjections, short noises in their throats. After the songs, one girl gave a testimony of how she had suffered in the bush but had now been given a chance to live like any other child.

Uncle Kim then introduced the choir as former child soldiers that the Wakisa Organisation had taken on. "We are trying to give them a chance at a new life," he explained. We all looked sad as we listened to him. And so did the audience. Uncle Kim then gave directions to the venue where we would perform the full show later that night, just in case anyone was interested in us and our music. We sang one more song, which we finished to thunderous applause from the audience. We bowed and then waved as we walked to our bus. We left amidst loud chatter and curious whispers. It was obvious that we were going to sing to a packed hall that night.

And we did.

#

Compared to what we had endured in the bush, we had found the Wakisa Children's Homes heavenly. We roamed freely on the spurring hills that housed the school and a large playground. For once I got to experience the delights of childhood. Though I was ten years old, I was allowed to be a child at Wakisa Children's Homes. Each home in the village had eight children and a mother looking after them. Ours was called Mum Helen. She was a beautiful lady. I loved her hands. They were strong and once in a while she grabbed me and tickled and we both giggled and squealed. Her hands were gentle. Her smile lit up my world. I think she must have been purposely chosen for me. In my world, she was mine alone. I did not share her with anyone. I and a boy I knew from the bush, who was called Rocky, had been put together in the same house with two other boys and four girls.

Martin, at twelve, was the oldest. Rocky was eleven, Robert ten, and I had just turned ten. The girls were between five and seven years old. Each of the children in the village had eight sponsors to fund their feeding, education, medical care, clothes, and discipleship.

On Sundays, we all gathered in the main hall for prayers. Wakisa was a Christian organization and although children of all faiths were accepted, the administrators emphasized Pentecostal beliefs and each of us was required to get saved. Some children allowed themselves to be saved for their own convenience: it was referred to as "becoming a *mulokole*." For me, it was all strange. I was born in the bush, without a religion. God and salvation were foreign concepts to me. At Wakisa, we were taught that there was a God who loved us and who was particularly interested in what we did with our lives. I felt too young to understand the whole thing. Nevertheless, I had to attend church service and I loved the part where the children danced and sang. They also gave testimonies of what God had done in their lives. It was quite entertaining. And after prayers we went back home to a delicious lunch of meat, rice and matooke. In the afternoon we would come back to the main hall to watch the Sunday movie. It was for those reasons that I loved Sunday. It was the best day of the week.

63

After a year in the children's village, a boy we knew from the bush and a girl joined us. The boy's name was Okello and the girl was Athieno. We were pleasantly surprised. Apparently all had not gone as well as expected in their families. They had suffered rejection and poverty. Desperate to find a better way, they had run back to the IDP camps and the camp authorities had sought help for them. Because of their ages, it had been hard to find any organisation that would take them in; they were both in their teens. An appeal was finally made to Wakisa Children's Homes, which accepted under the "Child Soldier No More" programme.

Of all the homes that the Wakisa Organization had, our village was chosen. Okello and Athieno were each placed in a different house. We were happy to be reunited.

"This is good, buddy," I said, as I hugged Okello.

"More than any of us had ever dreamt of!"

Athieno came forward and we hugged. "It is good to see you again, brothers," she said.

This is lovely!" Rocky said as he and Athieno hugged.

The new arrivals slid back into their role of big brother and big sister and Rocky and I were happy to show them around and talk to them about how Wakisa village life ran. They were able to fit in, and each found a different set of friends, although we still met occasionally because of the shared history that bound us. A history that no other child could understand.

#

That night in Japan, the curtains opened and *boom!* we appeared on stage. The girls jumping up and down, ululating, the boys bunching their muscles like their lives depended on it. We were doing the *laraka raka* dance from northern Uganda. The drummers followed, beating the drums till it seemed that they

64

would burst. Whatever we did, we did with energy and passion, as if it was the last thing we would ever do in this life. We sang from the depth of our souls, danced with our whole beings, grateful for the opportunity we had been given, the chance to live again. The audience loved it.

Doing a tour was one way of raising funds for the organisation. It was a gruelling four months on the road; the schedule was insane and the distances, miles upon miles, backbreaking. We did most of our travelling on buses. We ate, napped, slept, and played on the bus, much to the chagrin of our Uncles and Aunties who needed some peace after all the hard hours. Their work on the team was to look after us. They sacrificed a lot to see that everything went smoothly. It must have been difficult, for they were on duty twenty-four hours, seven days a week, four months on the road. With no reward except a weekly stipend doled out sparingly. Most used it to shop for things that would help them forget the long hours.

Sometimes our Uncles and Aunties had to discipline us. The serious cases were reserved for Uncle Kim. One day, a boy stole from a host's home. Uncle Kim took him back to say sorry. It was terrible for the rest of us. We did not want to witness it but we had to. The boy was not allowed any gifts till we returned to Uganda. But all in all, our Uncles and Aunties were our heroes. Their patience and kindness were way beyond what we had witnessed in our former lives.

Before the tour, our choir was trained in dance, drama, song, and stage presentation. It was intense. We had to sacrifice eight months of the school year to be able to do a tour. We had schoolbooks on the road and our Aunties and Uncles tried teaching us but it wasn't as conducive as the classroom. Being out of school was fun though. Which ten-year-old wouldn't consider it an adventure to travel to Japan? It was the biggest, happiest adventure of my life so far.

I remember the day when our tour started. We flew first to Dubai on Kenya Airways and changed to Cathay Pacific all the way to Hong Kong, from where we took our flight to Narita airport. Narita is a big airport and quite fancy. We could see it from the sky before we even landed because it glowed. It turned out to be my favourite of all the airports we had gone through, making our Entebbe Airport small and plain by comparison.

However, on arrival, Japan proved to be a dismal affair. The officials at the airport in their navy-blue pants and light-blue shirts pointed at us and laughed in disbelief. We must have amused them. Eighteen black children in grey sweat shirts! They asked for our letter of invitation to Japan, which Uncle Kim gave them. After they had scrutinized it as well as our visas, we were allowed to go through the security scanner one by one.

If our reception at the airport left more to be desired, our stay in Japan was altogether a different matter. The choir was well received. We performed to packed auditoriums, from Tokyo to Nagoya, Osaka to Hiroshima and then to Yokohama. We visited the atomic bomb memorial at Hiroshima. We were taken through the fateful day of August 6, when Americans dropped the deadly bomb on Japanese soil, altering the course of the Second World War. It was depressing walking through the museum. It reminded me of my time under Lomoki's rebel movement as a child soldier. The smell of human blood, bones, and death.

Our trips to Japanese schools were quite unsettling. The kids acted like we were the strangest beings ever created and stealthily poked at our black skins, which most children on the team found insulting. They had never seen black people before. Also, only a few of the Japanese schoolchildren could speak a bit of English, making communication next to impossible. We ended up using sign language most of the time.

Then there was the endless act of removing shoes. Japanese take off shoes and wear special sandals when entering places like gyms, classroom, theatres and homes. Their baths are also communal. And I can't forget that all the times we slept in hotels, we hardly slept on beds at all but pallets on the floor, which I found strange. Young as I was, I could tell that most Japanese were very polite and reserved. They edged towards shyness. Uncle Kim said they were conformists. I didn't know what it meant but when I asked him later, he said: *It is tough being different in Japan. You have to do things the way other people do them or risk being an outcast.*

When we talked to audiences, we emphasized forgiveness through our stories as the virtue that had helped us recover, that enabled us to live normal lives. I think most people went away with the desire to forgive someone in their lives. If we could forgive, so could any other person.

#

Our tour of Japan ended successfully. On the way to Osaka airport, we reminisced about all we had seen on our four-month journey. The wonderful and the disturbing. Gifts were given to the best performers, girl and boy. Although I did not win "Best Boy," I got a gift for having been the most helpful and obedient boy on the tour.

"Welcome home, my sons," Mother Helen said as she embraced me and Rocky at Entebbe Airport. I was happy to tell her of our tour during the bus ride to the villages, but I noticed that Rocky was not so eager.

Coming back from a fast world to the relaxed and boring village life was excruciatingly difficult. Adjusting to the rhythm of the village took longer than I had imagined. Things would never be the same again for me. I had picked up new habits of cleanliness, neatness and punctuality. Maintaining these was not easy. I had also got new knowledge, that I had value. I was a human being full of potential and talents that, if well developed, would enrich my world.

Before the tour, I thought I knew what the world was. But my perception of it had changed. From then onwards I could no longer live as though I was the only one in my world, the only one to have suffered and endured hard times. Despite the flashy life in Japan, I had been to homes that were dirty and poor; families that were broken and dysfunctional. I had seen children my age dealing in drugs, and older men living a life without a purpose. I had seen it all and it made me appreciate my homeland despite the war, disease and poverty.

Mother Helen was happy to have us back, but I now realised that she was backward and ignorant. Yet her love and warmth were irreplaceable, nothing could ever compare to the love she had for us. It was pure, strong and consistent. Rocky wasn't as lucky as me; he didn't think like I did. He wanted to live as though he were still on tour. He never snapped out of his fantasy. He was always in trouble with the other family members, and was rude and unkind to the girls especially. Soon, the labels "rebellious" and "difficult" became his around the village. After a year of conflict with Mother Helen, he was sent off to another house. It was sad watching him leave.

He wasn't the only one who failed to fit in after the tour; there were other boys and girls. The administration didn't do much to help them adjust; they assumed it was only a matter of time before they settled back into their old lives.

It took me two years to put the Japanese tour behind me. Standing at the back of my classroom, all the surrounding villages would be mine to savour. I still see the flower-farming shelters in the distance, the spread of the village farm, and the rich people's homes dotting the village perimeter. *What would I be? What would I become?* were the questions that plagued my mind. I was trying to connect my past to the present and the future. The person I had become and the person I was yet to be. That person waiting for me, I could only meet one day at a time. While on tour, I would introduce myself to our audience as follows, "Hello my name is Andrew Okumu and when I grow up, I want to be a teacher." The audience clapped.

As I stood and watched the village, I wasn't so sure anymore that I wanted to be a teacher. My voice was starting to break and there was hair growing under my arms and in my groin. There were also pimples on my face. I was no longer small. I was tall, with broad shoulders, but I still remained lean thanks to my fascination with basketball. Girls' bottoms and breasts fascinated me more than class work. So one day I asked a girl in my class called Halima to meet me next to a mango tree behind the school.

"Halima, you know you are cute," I told her when we were alone.

"What about it?"

"You and I can become an item."

"I am fine without being added to you to become an item."

"You know what I am talking about."

69

"No, I don't."

"You could be my girlfriend."

"Your girlfriend?"

"Yes, I mean it that way."

"I will think about it."

She thought about it long enough to dispel my interest. While a child soldier, it had been easy to get sex, even though boys as young as I was then were not allowed. I had done it a hundred times but those were now memories I wanted to erase from my mind. However excited I would get seeing a girl shake her bottom, just remembering sex in the bush killed my excitement. Yet, when I wasn't fighting those memories, it was a welcome distraction to think about sex. Our class teacher, during a sex education lesson, had warned us of the dangers of premarital sex, emphasizing the deadly AIDS. That had scared me enough. Although I still looked at Halima longingly, I knew I didn't want to die or become a father just yet. I wanted to complete my studies first.

Sex education did not help Rocky at all. At seventeen, he went after every girl that would give it to him, focusing his attention on the young girls who he knew could not get pregnant.

"Rock," I said him to one day when we met in the compound.

"What's up, Oks?" He called me Oks, short for Okumu.

"I am OK, buddy. I just want to talk to you."

"Hope it's not crap. I hate crap these days. Half the time crap is all that people have to say."

"You know me better. Tell me, where we can talk in peace? You and me alone, for old times' sake."

70

"We can talk behind my school block after class."

Rocky was there when I arrived. Not wanting to waste any time, I started. "Rock, we have come a long way and yet it seems that nothing binds us together anymore. You're not the boy I used to know."

"No, I'm not that boy, Oks. And neither are you."

"I miss the old Rock."

"No, I don't. I like the new Rock who is not scared of anything. Master of himself and controller of his own destiny."

I looked at him more closely. His eyes were sunken and bloodshot. The smell of liquor emanated from his crimped lips. For the first time, I noticed the emptiness in his eye. Contrary to what he said, I saw a boy who was barely in control of his destiny.

"I am proud of you and wish you well, but nothing binds us together anymore. And maybe nothing ever did," Rock said.

Before I could respond, he stood up and walked away. I felt a lump in my throat. It was then I knew I could not stomach the idea of losing him. I had to reclaim him at whatever cost.

One Sunday morning, Rocky sought me out and handed me a letter and said: "Read it! Maybe you will understand why I have taken the path I have taken." Then he strode away. I opened the letter.

Dear Andrew,

Growing up; you know how it was. No one ever told me what was wrong or right except that I had to kill to live. Many things happened to us, things that the outside world cannot understand. I am not strong like you. By the way, I am so proud of what you have become. Congratulations! My sensitive nature left me little room for stamina and endurance. What I endured in the bush was enough in itself.

71

When I had to deal with more, the hypocrisy of the world just curved in on me.

I have a confession. While you and other kids were being safely tucked into bed by Uncles and Aunties, my Uncle was busy molesting me. Making me do things that even the bush with all its madness had never forced me do! Uncle Kim raped me repeatedly and opened a new world of pain. He forbade me to tell anybody, saying I would be expelled from Wakisa if I dared do so. He threatened me with many other things. Being in a foreign country and always on the move, there was no way I could gather the courage to tell anyone. The betrayal of the closeness we had shared as Uncle and child was overwhelming. Did he know that I wanted to be like him? That he was my hero?

It all started one night in Tokyo. After we said goodnight to our host, Uncle Kim told me that I was going to share a bed with him. Once in his room, I wore my pyjamas while he showered. I was already in bed by the time he finished. He asked me to get out because he wanted to tuck me in properly. He said, "Paul, let me show you the right way a boy like you should be tucked in."

Yes, Uncle Kim, I answered as I jumped out.

Once on my feet, he removed my pyjamas. When I stood completely naked before him, he started rubbing my penis in a strange way. The rest I won't describe. But searing pain went through my behind as he pushed his thing in me. The pain penetrated my soul and left a wound so deep, it bleeds every time I recall that night. Later, when he was finished, he rubbed salted water where he had ravaged me and gave me painkillers and said I would be fine. Then he tucked me in and said, "Now, that is the best way to tuck a boy in. It should only remain between us, the rest of the boys and Uncles must never know."

The next day he informed everybody on the team that I was unwell. Maybe you remember that day when I remained indoors. He lied that I had been to the doctor and that I would be fine. Within two days I was OK, until he started it all over again. I endured the pain and the shame and he made it up to me by buying me toys and clothes. The tour ended but so did my dreams. There was no one I could trust to share my shameful secret with. And would anyone believe me anyway? That is when I decided I was different from the rest of the children. Oks, I do the things I do to numb the pain that I carry with me. I forgave Lomoki and his generals for the things they made us do in the bush. But, you see, Lomoki is generally acknowledged as a wicked man. If he did any wicked thing, the world wouldn't be surprised – but Uncle Kim? He is a Christian serving the lord diligently, preaching sinners out of hell. He is sanctified, and fire-spitting. Tell me. How do I forgive a person like Uncle Kim? He does not need my forgiveness. He is pure and holy while I, I am a child of the bush whose parent's grave is not even marked. A broken jar, a broken life, I need my vices. They keep me sane. Maybe someday, I will find a permanent balm for this ball of pain in my chest. Until then,

> *Yours,*
>
> *Rocky*

After reading his letter, I stared at the page in disbelief. Tears blurred my eyes; I wept for Rocky! Someone had messed him up! Again! He had fallen into a world of hopelessness and fear. I knew that world very well. It was all I had known a few years before. What could I do to help him? His letter opened up a world that was not easy to talk about. No one except us — former child soldiers — would endure what Rocky had gone through. We had to bear it because we needed to go to school, to feed, and we also needed a place to lay our heads. Where else could we go? I felt overwhelmed by it all. Helpless and timid, I acknowledged my lack of courage to face it, and that is the worst feeling I have ever had to deal with.

I started noticing other things too. Things I had not paid much attention to until recently. How conveniently other programs had been abandoned as soon as it was realized that a tour of child soldiers could bring in more money. Adult supervision in the homes was also noticeably absent. We had too much time on our hands, making it easy for young children and teenagers to turn to vice. Sex was called "painting," and many of the children did just that and a whole lot more.

I also saw for the first time Mother Helen's struggles in the home. I, Robert and Martin were already in our teens, and Rocky, having proved to be too much for her to handle, had already left. The girls had entered their teens as well, and had started behaving irresponsibly. How could she be a mother to all of us with all our difficult backgrounds? Didn't she have a life of her own, children of her own? She cared for us with devotion and it was that love that held us together. She was the rock, the centre. She was the ground under our feet. But who took care of her?

Okello, surprisingly, did very well in his studies and got a government scholarship to study medicine at Makerere University. Athieno was not so lucky. She had blossomed into a beautiful young woman and although she and Okello had once been an item, she had forgotten him like a bad dream. But university didn't go well for her. She hooked up with a rich man who dumped her as soon as she got pregnant. She eventually graduated from Makerere, but with no job offers coming in, she was forced to seek help from the village administration. Wakisa

74

did not let her down, and Okello, too, came to her rescue. After the baby was born, the two of them got married. It was the first wedding in Wakisa Children's Home and that is when I caught up with Rocky again. He came to attend the wedding. He looked calm, like someone had returned his peace of mind to him. I was dumbfounded to see him.

"What's up buddy?' He asked as soon as he caught sight of me.

"Not much, Rock, good to see you again. You left us just like that!"

"Yes, I did."

"It wasn't proper, man."

"I know, I know, but it's nice to see you again. So much has happened since."

"You are looking good."

"Oh, I do?"

"I am curious—how you did it?"

"Long story . . . I will talk to you later. But did you receive my letter?"

"Which letter?"

"Never mind. We'll talk. I have a few days here after this wedding."

He walked forward to congratulate the bride and groom, leaving me to follow. As soon as Rocky turned away, Okello drew me aside and told me he had my letter. "I will give it to you later. After this madness. Rocky gave it to me a few months ago when I met him."

"But where did you meet him? You never said a word!" I said, but more people were waiting their turn to hug the *new couple*.

Through the rest of the day I was thinking about the letter. I wondered what else Rocky had wanted me to know. Early the next morning, I was at the door of the newlyweds honeymoon chamber. Okello opened the door a crack and thrust the envelope at me. I waited until I was back in my room before I tore it open.

Dear Andrew,

I hope all is well with you. The last time I wrote I was walking in darkness so deep, but I am now happy to write that things have changed for the better. Shortly after I handed you the letter, Uncle Kim invited me to his office in Kampala. I didn't want to see him, but I went out of curiosity and the fact that he was an authoritative figure in our lives. I could not disobey.

"It is nice to see you, Paul," he said when I entered his office. I didn't answer him. He pointed to a seat opposite, and I sat. "I have heard a lot about your misdemeanours and, you will agree with me, we have given you many chances to turn a new leaf," he said, staring at me as he spoke.

I still said nothing. After what seemed an eternity of silence from my end, Uncle Kim rose, moved round his desk, and stood in front of me. He looked at me sternly, before he asked, "Does your behaviour have anything to do with what happened between us on the Japanese tour?"

Looking straight at him, I said, "I have nothing to say to the man who ruined my life!"

"Your life was already ruined long before I came on the scene. You should be grateful — I gave you a chance at a new life."

"I am a mess, thanks to that chance," I said.

"Do you honestly think you would have done much better if we had not taken you in?"

"I don't know, but I am sure I would not have been assaulted by a homosexual masquerading as a born-again pastor!"

"Get out of my office!" he bellowed.

"With pleasure," I replied.

I don't know what Uncle Kim did, but the next thing I knew, I was on a plane bound for the USA. He sent me to an elderly couple who enrolled me into a therapy clinic. My doctor was nice and encouraged me to face my pain and forgive Uncle Kim. It was similar to what we had been told in the rehabilitation centre at Pader. The elderly couple, Martin and Elise, loved me very much and decided to accept me as their son and that is where I have been since. I severed all communication with Uncle Kim and when my new parents ask me about him, I just say I don't know much. And I don't want to know.

Now I am happy. I have forgiven Kim. But the world is a school, my brother. Our world is a school.

I came back as soon as I got the news about Okello and Athieno's wedding. I had to come and see my buddies.

So long.

Your brother,

Rocky.

I folded the letter and tucked it in my pocket. I was more dumbfounded by the letter than I had been by seeing the man at the wedding.

Later in the day, I and Rocky linked up for coffee at Antonio's. We had a lot to talk about, but we barely spoke. Rocky was on his way to becoming an American citizen. I was happy for him. As for me, I am still stuck in a children's village. I am a teacher here, but my dreams are growing bigger every day. I am becoming a man.

77

Chasing Butterflies

Colleen Higgs

Joburg is unseasonably hot, and Jake is squashed into a small table on the pavement at Nino's in Braamfontein, his favourite lunch spot, just up the hill from Wits University. He is meeting his friend Alice for lunch. Jake wants to persuade Alice that she and her young family should emigrate. He thinks about emigrating every day. He doesn't hold out much hope for the future in this country, this continent.

At 70 though, he isn't sure if it matters for him. It's more of the idea of a better life elsewhere, a "grass is greener" sort of idea. He worries about Alice and her idealistic husband, Harold, who works for a land claims NGO, almost in the same way that he worries about his own daughter, Emma, who also works for an NGO, an EU HIV/AIDS outfit in Kampala. He wishes Emma had chosen a more mainstream life, and he also wishes that she would find a suitable man to have children with. Instead, she lives what he sees as a makeshift sort of life, without what he considers a proper home, although he would be the last to tell her. He is aware that she probably knows what his views are. He hopes that life will be kind to both Emma and Alice, but he isn't optimistic.

Hunched over the *Guardian Weekly*, one of several foreign newspapers and magazines he subscribes to, Jake is reading an article about the new pope. How on earth could they have chosen this Ratzinger fellow? He takes it as a personal affront. "What about all those Catholics who will continue to be told not to use condoms, even though they're married and have several children?" he mutters. "Married women are the most at risk." He worries about the women at risk from HIV infection, from physical abuse; the married ones, the single, the old.

"It's like chasing butterflies, all the things you worry about, Jake," Alice said to him one day.

Alice reminds him of his wife, Susan, who died at forty-five. She is earnest and kind, and unaware of the impression she makes on others. She laughs easily and he enjoys her company, she is a breath of fresh air in his life. She is in her late thirties, about the same age as Emma is now, and as jolly as Susan was when she died. Whatever the reason, he likes her enormously. It is an undemanding friendship. He met Alice in the lift in the building he worked in, when he first moved to Joburg ten years ago. She still lived in Yeoville and wasn't married then. Now she consults for the City Council, which offers her the flexibility to raise children.

Alice and Jake started talking the first day they met and within a fortnight they were meeting for lunch most weeks, picking up on their conversation as though there hadn't been a break. He's listened to her tales of woe about several unsuitable relationships, and more recently to her reports of the trials and tribulations of small children, her tricky if tactful mother-in-law, the vagaries of her own mother's mental health, as well

80

as innumerable other minor domestic dramas. He usually has some useful counsel for her, or at least an impartial opinion, which Alice values.

She rushes in, fifteen minutes late, and starts talking before she has even sat down. Every time he sees her she is in the midst of a new crisis. "He made a pass at me; well I think that's what it was. He was squeezing my shoulders, sort of massaging them. Thank God my cell phone rang! I grabbed my bag and didn't even switch my computer off . . ." She orders a cappuccino and the *penne arabiatta*, as she tells Jake about her current client's latest outrage. "I mean who does he think he is? It's not as though he doesn't know I'm married, he's had dinner with Harold and me for God's sake. I can't understand him. What on earth was he thinking of? What about his wife? I'm so furious I could punch something. Why does he think he can get away with something like this?"

Before she has finished spilling out her woes, the waitress interrupts with their orders. His is a chicken *tramezzino*; he eats it all, putting down the triangles in between bites. He touches her arm gently before saying, "I would just ignore it. You aren't going to get anywhere taking it up as a grievance. It is awkward though, isn't it?" They debate this and other issues while they eat, Jake looking around as though appealing to an imaginary audience, a habit from his days as a university teacher. He flings his hands around as he talks. He is an attractive man at 70, his athletic build makes him look like a long-distance runner, but his hair, with its wild and wiry whiteness, gives his age and disposition away.

The only time he was nearly unfaithful to Susan comes to mind suddenly. He had been working late, hoping the Dean would call to let him know if he had been promoted to Head

81

of Department. He still remembers how his desk looked that night: stacks of books, unmarked exam papers in a teetering pile, the wax crayon drawing of herself as a princess that Emma had done in primary school tacked to his pin board. He'd been staring into the middle distance for several minutes. Just as he decided to pack it in for the evening, and was pulling on his coat, Mary, one of his graduate students, came into his office.

"Please could you look at my results when you have a chance? There's something I'm not seeing. I need another perspective." Mary stood in the door. Beyond her the lab was empty and dark; the others had gone home. Both her hands were deep in the pockets of her jeans as she leaned back against the doorframe, her feet slightly apart, and she stared at him through her thick dark hair. Jake looked past her, like a dog trying to find a way out of a tight spot.

"Uh, sure, let's talk about it tomorrow. I have to dash now."

She smiled, lowering her eyes. "Come and have a quick drink at the Sunnyside, it's on your way."

"No, I can't, not tonight. I'm afraid I have to go now. I'll have a look at your . . . um, results tomorrow. First thing." As she stepped away from the door and moved towards him, he coughed nervously and jingled his keys in his pocket.

"Not even one?"

She was now close enough for him to smell her excitement. He sighed. He had been aware of her, this girl, woman, younger than his own daughter, for months now. He had yearned for her, her eager bright mind, her gleaming skin and her hair that he longed to take in his hands and bury his face in. Susan was sick for many months before she died.

82

"No."

"Another time?"

"Hm. Yes, another time." He smiled, and reached behind her to switch off the light.

As he drove home from the university that night, he thought about the night Emma was born, how he paced up and down that bleak hospital corridor. In those days, fathers weren't expected to be in delivery rooms — in fact, they weren't allowed in them. Now you're considered inhuman if, God forbid, you don't want to attend the birth of your child. I was only twenty-four; we did it all so much earlier then. After that everything became blurry, as though he was on a fairground horse, going round and round, faster and faster. He remembers seeing Emma for the first time, she was so odd and otherworldly, her face a bit squashed, but because she was his, he fell in love with her right away. Susan was tired, her hair damp, but she was smiling as though she'd won a race. She was so full of belief and good will, a bit like Alice.

He thinks of Emma again as he watches Alice finish her cappuccino. They always split the bill. He fishes in his pocket for coins for the tip, after peering at the bill for a moment. "I wouldn't worry too much," he says, patting Alice's back. "If the moment passed, it passed. Just keep out of his way for a bit, especially after dark, or after he's had a lunch meeting, and a couple of glasses of chardonnay." He smiles conspiratorially at her.

Alice swirls her soft tangerine-coloured scarf around her neck as she gathers herself together. "You're right. Of course you're right." She kisses him gently on the cheek. "I'm not going back there today . . . he can stuff off," she calls as she breezes out of Nino's and round the corner. It puts him in mind of trees rustling on an otherwise still day.

83

Torpedo

Constance Obonyo

"Gabudieri, wipe those tears from your face immediately!" his father would roar from his perch on a wooden stool in the compound, his arms raised above his head, ready to strike. "Men never cry!" And whenever his father found him sharing a joke with the girls in the neighbourhood, he would order, "Away from those girls! A man is supposed to be strong, to show no emotion. That is how we separate the men from the boys." Gabudieri was tired of it all. A man must not do this, must not do that, must not do anything.

It became worse when the government passed a law on sterilising circumcision tools because of the threat of HIV/AIDS. "You should not have been born during this time, Gabudieri. Back in the day, men were men. A man would not so much as blink as the knife sliced through him. Men who showed pain were a disgrace. But now, we have to sterilise knives!" He would shake his head in disgust. "A real man knows no disease."

Because of Gabudieri's light, smooth skin and small hands and feet, the boys at school teased him. "Cissy!" they would shout, causing Gabudieri embarrassment.

85

In his first year of secondary school, he started writing his name as Gabriel. Gabudieri will not do here, he said to himself. So Gabriel he became. His father however insisted on calling him Gabudieri. "That was your grandfather's name and you must respect his memory by using his name," his father said one day, with a pained expression. "And my father was a hardworking man. With your lazy legs that drag like an earthworm, I do not see you become like him."

"I have heard you, father. Can I go now?" was his response. It was all so annoying. He decided to prove his father wrong.

#

"Will you need these, sir?" Amon, Gabriel's personal assistant, peered round the door, nervous. He was holding a stack of four manila files.

"Which ones are those? Are they the ones I told you to look for this morning?" Gabriel asked from behind his large, polished, oak desk. The question was curt. He glared at Amon.

"The Southern By-pass Road Project," Amon said in a cowed voice.

Gabriel studied him for a moment. "Amon, how can you bring me those files now? I asked for them as soon as I entered this office this morning. What have you been doing all day?" His voice shook with anger.

Amon's voice faltered. "I had to type up the report you said was urgent. I had to look for these. I could not find them at first . . ."

"*Eh, eh!* Give them over." He gestured for the files and dismissed Amon with an angry wave of the hand. "What are you waiting for? Go!"

86

Amon slipped from the room, closing the door behind him. Gabriel stared at the door for some time, his anger ebbing away. *Amon has only recently started work,* he thought. *I shouldn't be too hard on him.* Amon had been referred to him by a friend. Since he had no work experience, employing him had been a favour.

Gabriel regarded the files on his desk with a wary look. He had to go home and get some rest. He decided to take the work home. His cell phone let out its shrill ringtone.

"Hello, Benjy? How are you? No . . . I am sorry I will not be able to come today . . . I am too tired; I need to rest. I'm also taking some work home . . . I know. Of course I haven't got a wife to tie me down . . . I am married to my work. Yes, women can be a pain . . . I know. Anyway, enjoy yourselves. And please let me know what happens . . . OK."

Gabriel ended the call and stood up. He was six foot two inches tall. His black hair contrasted with his light skin. He was quite big in the chest and shoulder, thanks to his many visits to the gym. He had the carriage of a model. Most people considered him attractive. At thirty-eight, many had started wondering why he was still unmarried.

#

Gabriel reached for the plaque on his desk and turned it around. *Eng. Gabriel Sibo, PhD.,* it read. He was proud of his achievements.

His father was long dead. He knew his father would have been proud of what his son had achieved, at least to some extent. He would not have been happy that his Gabudieri had exchanged marriage and children for a career, but that would have been understandable. Sure there had been mishaps in his private life, but his achievements overshadowed them all. In any

87

case, Dorcas, his first girlfriend, had been too immature for him. All she could talk about was teddy bears, fashionable clothes, and hairstyles. And yet she was a university undergraduate. She had to go.

Phillipa had been good looking and intelligent. They had been in university together. In fact, everyone who knew them thought they were a well-matched couple. But he felt nothing for her and did not foresee a happy future with her. In fact, she was too clingy and had wanted to tie him down with children while he was still chasing his career goals. The girl needed to get a life. Despite his friends' heated protests, she had to go.

After university, many had come and gone. Jolly had moved into his flat briefly after he got his first job. But she, too, soon found a job, hooked up with other corporate types and started hanging out with the girls till late. She started domestic battles about everything. She wanted him to make the bed when he was the last to get out of it. She wanted him to share the cooking and the cleaning. She had even drawn up a roster.

One day when he had forgotten to wash his underwear she had moaned about it on facebook until the whole of Kampala was following the woes of their relationship. She never touched a saucepan, and when he once requested that she prepare something special for him, she declared him a chauvinist. She accused him of not wanting her to have any help around the house, and of wanting her to prepare his meals personally. She had to go.

Several misfit girlfriends later, Gabriel decided to concentrate on career advancement. After getting a doctorate degree and starting a successful engineering company, he seemed to have achieved his dreams. He maintained a skeleton staff at his offices and hired experts whenever he had big projects. His company — which specialized in road construction — grew from strength to strength.

In the first ten years, the company carried out small road maintenance projects. But as the reputation of the company grew, the government started inviting them to bid for major construction projects. It was a big breakthrough when they got the Southern By-pass Road Project. It was a much-talked-about project. Television stations and newspapers interviewed Gabriel at every opportunity. He became a household name. Traffic congestion in Kampala was such a nuisance that residents welcomed the project with excitement.

So, when the project started to unravel, to fall apart, Gabriel was part and parcel of that unravelling. The survival of his company was at stake.

#

Early the next morning, Gabriel was back at his desk. He spoke into the intercom. "Amon, can I have a bottle of water please?"

"Yes, sir," came the reply.

"Thank you, Amon," Gabriel said a few moments later. He stared at the closing door as the younger man left the room. It had been ten good years and he and his small staff had managed to keep the company afloat. But I wonder where he will go and what he will do when he finds out, poor Amon, he thought.

His Blackberry had been ringing all morning, but he ignored most of the calls. Now, after the phone stopped ringing, he reached for it, steeled himself, and dialled the lawyer's number for the third time that morning.

"Mr. Mukwaya, are you ready? Shall I come now?"

"Mr. Sibo, I will call you as soon as the judge is ready. It is a mess, but we should be able to get over some hurdles today, so that you can go away for some time. We need to get you an Official Receiver at the High Court, who will deal with it all. When you are declared bankrupt, you will be as free as a bird. No more creditors. Be patient, alright?"

"Alright. Are you sure the media has not got wind of it yet?"

"Yes, I am sure. We are going to be safely out of the way by the time they get to know. I have arranged a safe hideaway. You do not have to say anything. Leave the media to me. We shall arrange a statement for them. I will call shortly." Mr. Mukwaya disconnected the call before Gabriel could continue with his nervous questions.

Mr. Mukwaya called half an hour later. He had arranged for an army-green Land Cruiser to convey Gabriel to the High Court. Gabriel emerged from his plush office on the fourth floor of Workers' House in the calmest manner he could manage. He addressed his personal assistant. "Amon, if anyone calls, I am out on business."

"Yes, sir," Amon replied without so much as a glance in his direction. He was typing on his computer.

Gabriel walked out of the office with steady strides. He wore a white shirt and plain red tie under a black Armani suit. Swinging his black briefcase, he walked into the blue-carpeted corridor and pushed a button to call the lift. He was alone. Everyone is busy at their desks, he thought miserably. His palms were sweaty and his stomach churned. His bladder was full but he decided not to indulge it.

The lift arrived. Two women—one in a black velvet suit, white silk blouse and black shoes, the other in a navy-blue work suit, light pink blouse and blue shoes—stared at him from inside the lift. He hesitated, and then strode in. They made room for him. He pushed the "G" button.

It was not difficult to pick out the car Mr. Mukwaya had sent. He climbed into the backseat, and the journey to the High Court began. It was not a long distance away, but the journey felt like a thousand miles.

Everything happened so quickly. He found Mr. Mukwaya waiting for him at the bottom of the stairs to the courtroom. Mr. Mukwaya ushered him into an office, where they paid some fees. The judge was already seated in the courtroom, and after they took their seats, the proceedings began. Gabriel answered the judge's questions mechanically, with a few promptings now and then from Mr. Mukwaya. It was soon over and he returned to the cool interior of the Land Cruiser, followed by his lawyer. The outcome of the hearing was that an Official Receiver was appointed to handle his bankruptcy petition.

"Drive straight to the airport," Mr. Mukwaya whispered to the driver. He leaned into the open window and smiled at Gabriel, who was seated behind the driver. "Don't worry. Everything will be settled in due course. Stay down there for a while. I will call you." He pushed a copy of John Grisham's *The Firm* into Gabriel's sweaty palms, and then waved the driver away.

Later, as he settled into his hotel room in faraway Kidepo Valley National Park, he wondered what was happening in Kampala, whether the news had already broken and whether his photo would be on television. He sank his head into the soft white pillow and let the tears flow.

He cried himself to sleep.

91

The Southern By-pass Road Project had been mismanaged. Money had disappeared. The road, which was supposed to be a superhighway consisting of twelve lanes, six on both sides, was only half the size, with several essential layers missing from the road surface. It was supposed to have been commissioned the year before, but several partners had been unhappy with the work. The public started asking questions, the donors grew annoyed. There were powerful people involved in the project, and they wanted scapegoats. So, to avoid a state scandal, the contractors, engineers and some civil servants were made examples of. The powerbrokers involved sent a pack of burly hooligans to the concerned parties to knock sense into their heads.

One night, Gabriel heard a gunshot. It sounded uncomfortably close. His flat on Nakasero hill shook from the sound. He had been watching the 9 o'clock news on NTV. He instinctively threw himself on the floor, his fall broken by the plush red wall-to-wall rug.

Rada, the houseboy, ran to the living room, switched off the lights and joined Gabriel on the floor. "You should never do that again," Gabriel whispered fiercely. "As soon as you hear a gunshot, just lie down wherever you are. It is dangerous to keep walking around!" Then they heard footsteps coming closer, approaching the front door. Gabriel stared at Rada in alarm. "Do you think they are armed robbers?" he whispered.

"Ooh . . . I hope not!" Rada whispered back. In the light that poured from the television, Gabriel noticed that Rada's eyes and teeth had become the most prominent features on his face. His coffee skin seemed to have melted into the surrounding darkness.

Suddenly the kitchen door flew open and four men burst into the room. Their torch beams swept the room and fell on the two men cowering on the floor. "*Shh!*" said one of the men, who seemed to be the leader. "Keep quiet and nobody gets hurt. Turn on the light and draw the curtains. Where is the switch?"

Rada clambered to his feet and switched on the light. "The curtains are drawn, sir," he said after he had seen to that.

"OK, you two cooperate with us and no one gets hurt. Do you understand?" the leader barked. He sat down on one of the cream velvet chairs and watched the two captives.

"What do you want . . . I can give you all the money I have . . ." Gabriel begged in a shaky voice, his hands stretched out in front of him.

"Shut up! I do the talking here. You listen!" the leader said, striking Gabriel's outstretched hands with the barrel of his gun. The barrel was shorter than a Kalashnikov. Gabriel figured it was a submachine gun. It looked more sophisticated than the guns the police carried. The four men all carried the same gun model, and all had rows of bullets criss-crossing their torsos. They wore black skin-tight clothing, with black balaclavas on their heads and black canvas shoes. Gabriel knew he was not going to survive their mission, whatever it was.

"We have not come for money," the leader said, and crossed his leg. "We have come to reach an understanding with you." He said this while prodding Gabriel's right cheek with his gun barrel. "The Southern By-pass, it is overdue for commissioning."

"Yes, sir," Gabriel said. "What do you want me to do?"

"Don't play dumb with me, man! Your watchman— *ntcha!*" He made a sign with his hand to indicate a beheading.

A sob escaped Gabriel. Tears streamed down his face. He had brought the watchman from his village.

"I don't know, man, whether you understand. That watchman out there, he is just a warning. You sing and you are dead! You, the contractors and a few other people, you've got to take the blame. Do you understand now? Otherwise, *ntcha!*" He demonstrated again what would befall Gabriel if he did not comply.

"I understand, sir."

"Fully?"

"Yes sir. Fully."

The man regarded him for some moments, then said, "Alright then. Pray that we will not meet again. Let this be the first and last warning." He said this as he tapped Gabriel's forehead with the barrel of his gun. Then he stood up and gestured to his boys. They filed out of the house.

Gabriel and Rada stayed in their positions for the next thirty minutes, fearing that the men would return. Then they rose from the floor and locked up the house. The night was endless. In the morning, Gabriel made several phone calls to the police. To explain the death of his watchman, he cooked up a story about armed robbers breaking into his house.

The assets of Sibo Engineering Consultants Ltd. could not cover the damages the court would award the state for the financial loss Gabriel's company was supposed to have caused. And to avoid the harassment of creditors, Gabriel filed for bankruptcy as an individual. The state would handle the bankruptcy of his ten-year-old company.

#

Gabriel spent the next two months at Kidepo. Mr. Mukwaya called every day to update him about the situation in Kampala. The only other person who knew his secret number was Pastor

Omoding. Sometimes he felt the pastor was hiding some information from him. He wondered what had been said about him, especially in the tabloids.

"Sibo Engineering and all the implicated companies and individuals cannot absorb the missing funds from the road project. That kind of financing can only come from an international bank. Do not blame yourself. It is unfortunate, but you have to get over it—pick up the pieces. It happens." Mr. Mukwaya had explained this to him when he wondered aloud why both he and his company had to file for bankruptcy.

Then one day, nine weeks after his flight from Kampala, Mr. Mukwaya called him and said: "You can leave that place now. I'll send the car. Where do you want to go?"

Gabriel hesitated. He could not go back to Sironko, where he grew up. Go back and do what? His father was long dead. All he would be meet there would be his childhood playmate Mundu and his father Mutende and their triumphant stares. So you thought you were so high and mighty? Look at you now, a penniless jobless village dweller like us.

He had not built a house in the village, something his father lamented about until his death. Was he going to live in a mud-and-wattle house? What about food, would he grow his own food? No way! But all his personal property and that of Sibo Engineering had been confiscated. He was poor, homeless. He had no choice.

Without anyone to recommend him for any engineering projects, he was grounded. The crooked government officials had made him look as dirty as possible, and no serious investor would touch him with the trunk of the highest tree in Mabira Forest. He was the dirty thief, the sacrificial lamb. I am grateful to be alive, of course, he thought to himself. I know a door will

95

surely open that none will dare close, not even the mafia. He reached for his phone and dialled Pastor Omoding's number. It was a new life, one with an unclear direction, but he was ready to begin.

The Fulani

Yaba Badoe

It's taken me a long time to tell you this story, but tell it I must. That's the way it is sometimes. You hold something back for as long as you can, then you begin to cough as it crawls up your throat, and unless you pull it out of your mouth with words, you will surely choke. My dilemma is how to begin a story that has never been told. There is the woman herself, the Fulani, transported from the town of Gambaga in the north of Ghana by my great-grandfather, an Nzema merchant. He adored her melodious voice, and her fierce, exuberant spirit he loved even more.

It would be easy to spin my yarn as a cross-cultural love story to complement our own: a village girl, accused of witchcraft, is saved from the enmity of her relatives by a rich southerner, who, taking compassion on her, rescues her from the witches' camp for which the town is famous and brings her down to the vibrant port city of Axim. But there is his first wife to contend with. She takes pity on the younger woman and gives her as a token of friendship the *ahweniee* she has made with precious aggrey beads from Togo and gold from the Ankobra River.

I could embroider a luminous tapestry threaded with love and tolerance, though in reality the stigma of witchcraft remained with the Fulani. As if to confirm her unnatural propensity, she died childless, and with neither sons nor daughters to protect her interests was laid to rest in the wild hinterland surrounding Axim. I am tempted to tell you all these things, but must speak quickly, if I must tell the whole tale.

I must have been about thirteen when I first saw the *ahweniee*. My mother, believing me old enough to wear her jewellery, invited me to her bedroom. We were getting ready for a family occasion—a wedding, maybe, or the naming ceremony of a new family member. I can't remember what we were celebrating, but I do recall that I was in a white lace cloth wrapped, Nigerian style, around my waist, and strutting about in my first pair of high heels. Mama, thinking I needed a special set of earrings to complement the elaborate head tie that crowned my outfit, unlocked her jewellery box.

She turned over her treasures: pendants and bracelets from my father, a sapphire brooch from a fellow writer; a pair of golden hoop earrings from a best friend at school. She related the stories behind each trinket she touched in her search to find what suited me best. There were gifts from my grandmother especially, and a gold crest from my father that her fingers lingered on. Beside it, tucked in a corner of the box, the coiled *ahweniee* glistened seductively.

"What's that?" I asked, reaching out for it.

"Don't touch it!" The arm my mother had draped around me dropped to her side, deflating the voluminous sleeves of her dress: a luxurious Senegalese *boubou* made from the same lace

98

as mine. Mama sighed, and as she shook her head, the loop of intimacy she had encircled me with tightened and gently she reeled me in.

The story she told of a woman discarded by family and friends, then rescued thanks to the radiant beauty of her voice, was enthralling and, although I gratefully accepted the pearl earrings Mama selected for me, I knew in my heart that it was the love-beads I was after.

I started badgering my grandmother for more information. Late one afternoon, we were sitting on the porch of her bungalow in Axim, having just finished lunch. The neighbours on either side of the house were preparing *fufu*, and the rhythmic thud and thump of wooden pestles pounding cassava punctuated our conversation. Nana's fingers jerked sporadically as she crocheted a white tablemat—yet another in the endless supply she produced for relatives.

"Nana," I began, "what do you know about the woman called the Fulani who married into our family a long time ago?"

My grandmother frowned.

"Why doesn't anyone talk about her? What did she do that was so bad that nobody mentions her name? Won't you even tell me her name?" I pleaded.

Shaking her head, Nana brought a finger to her lips and sniffing loudly between stitches, tut-tutted, then sighed as my mother had sighed, prefacing her disapproval with a "Hmmm": a sound that insinuated mysteries that were as likely to occur in this world as the one to come.

"Cuba," she admonished, "one day your questions will get you into trouble. Some things are best left alone."

"But why, Nana?"

My grandmother was as dark as my mother, with a velvet lustre to her skin that made her handsome face shine with an inner glow. A rotund, short woman who had traded in cloth for most of her life, her eyes were sharp and penetrating. In contrast, her wide, generous mouth failed to do justice to an implacable will. A pink silk scarf was tied around her grey hair, but her hairline, denuded after decades of plaiting with cotton thread, pulled away from the pink covering to reveal delicate strands of tiny hair.

"Hmmm," she reiterated, emphatically.

"Please tell me her story, Nana. It happened so long ago."

Nana grumbled a little longer. In the end, it appeared that by framing the inquiry as a story offended her less than if I'd persisted in asking for the bald facts of the Fulani's life. "May the good Lord protect us from evil," my grandmother murmured, so softly that I almost didn't hear. "May He protect us from spirits and demons intent on rupturing family ties," she whispered, sighing again. She rolled up the tablemat she had been working on, and let her hands rest for the first time that day as she fixed her gaze on me.

"My dear grandchild," she began in her gravest voice, "the Fulani came to us long ago as an outsider; she never learnt our songs, because the songs she yearned to sing were from a faraway kingdom in the north. But I heard her voice. We all did. Whenever she bathed and the spirit came to her, she couldn't stop herself singing. And she had such a beautiful voice: smooth and silky, like finely woven Kente cloth. The very best, mind you, the type they weave with gold thread for the Asantehene alone. She was unique. When the Fulani sang praise songs, my

100

dear, even the angels crying alleluia to God on high must have stopped what they were doing to sprinkle her with gold dust. Your great-grandfather certainly did. He loved her too much, that man. But in the end she went blind. Another sign, if any more were needed, that she was one of them."

"What do you mean, Nana?"

With her hands on her lap, my grandmother bent forward, her neck jutting out in horror: "Do I have to show my own grandchild how to suck milk from the breast? What is all your book learning for, Cuba, if you cannot understand African science? Born a witch, you die a witch," she declared. "Marrying the old man didn't change a thing, my dear. We learnt how to tolerate her, that's all. But we kept our distance. Even though she was kind to me, and I never went hungry while she was around, I would never sleep by her side at night. No, not beside that one!"

"Was she very beautiful, Nana?"

"Hmmm." My grandmother shook her head sadly. "You girl with your too many questions! What is beauty if your womb doesn't bear fruit? I was the old man's last-born, so when I came into the world, the Fulani was still young. But she was barren. The old man's love wasn't enough to conceive a child. She visited shrine after shrine to try to satisfy her gods, but nothing helped. Before she died, she cried: 'Who will bury me? Who will make sure they don't thrust thorns in my feet to prevent me returning? Who will pay for my funeral when I have no children of my own?' I promised that I would bury her. And I did. Yes," Nana whispered. "The Fulani was good to me. She was the most gentle of her kind in Axim, and there are more of them here than in the whole of Accra. Are you satisfied now, my grandchild?"

The Fulani's name hovered, unspoken, as a pained, haunted expression unsettled my grandmother's face, clouding her eyes.

"Did they put thorns in the soles of her feet to stop her coming back again?"

Nana chomped her jaws shut. The grim set of her mouth made it impossible to question her further. A mesh of unhappiness seemed to vibrate in the afternoon air. On one side was my grandmother and her memories, while on the other I stood alone, eager to glimpse the face and feet of the Fulani through Nana's eyes.

The next morning as I got ready for the journey home to Accra, I sensed the same tainted web of melancholy in the air, its filaments a tangle of undeclared secrets. I brooded over it, and before I could understand what was happening, it enveloped me. Interwoven with my thoughts was a thread of compassion for the Fulani. I pitied her. Yet a part of me, drawn to thinking of her as a heroine in a romantic novel, secretly revered her. Even more beguiling was the fact that no one I asked could disclose the exact nature of her original transgression; probably because no one, apart from the old man, had dared to enquire.

I was at an age when outlaw women of tragic erotic appeal were compelling. The Fulani wasn't exactly a role model. She wasn't even properly an ancestor since we weren't related by blood. However, her story captured my imagination to the extent that I sometimes dreamt of her singing at night, and in the morning woke with her music in my ears. So of course, when I fell for Isaiah, and he persuaded me to run away with him, it seemed right that I should take the *ahweniee* as a talisman. Once people trust you as much as my mother did back then, it is easy to steal from them.

#

I am not sure how much I can tell you, my love, before you start to see me as those others do: spiritually contaminated, damaged goods. Or worse still, a middle-aged spinster fixated on a teenage love affair. Please listen without interrupting me, without any hint of condemnation in your eyes.

Imagine a lagoon, a luxuriantly wild place where mangroves grow. And on the lagoon there is a sheltered island. That's where Isaiah and I camped out for over a week. He'd visited the lagoon with his uncle, and though he'd never set foot on it, he knew of the island. It was the home of a deity, a water spirit revered by local fishermen. We weren't supposed to be there, but we didn't give a damn. Isaiah's parents wanted him to become an engineer, even though he lived and breathed music. He wasn't having any of it, so he took off in protest. I tagged along.

The island appeared ideal for our escapade. The lagoon was teeming with fish and there were fruit trees: coconut palms, guava, a grove of oranges and avocados where we made our den. We woke early in the morning to the chatter of monkeys, the raucous laughter of birds, and at night, we watched cascades of shooting stars light up the sky, blissfully unaware that the spot we slept on was a shrine that we desecrated with our bodies. The place we called "home" was the deity's temple; the trees we plucked, her sacred grove.

Everything was fine the first week. Between fishing and fetching water from a spring on the other side of the lagoon, we played with the love-beads I'd strung around my waist. When he first saw them, Isaiah was apprehensive. They weren't the sort of thing middle-class girls wore, he claimed. He wasn't used to such adornments. He jiggled it, giggling nervously, my head cradled in the nook of his arm, his hand avoiding contact with my breasts. We were clumsy with the *ahweniee* and awkward with each other, until, inspired by his gift for music, Isaiah began to use me as a guitar he strummed with a song in his head, a drum he tapped to his own rhythm.

"Cause I'm a voodoo chile. Lord knows I'm a voodoo chile," he growled. Taking a deep breath, he created a backing track with instruments he imitated with his mouth, my forearm the sleek strings of his new guitar.

We tentatively explored our bodies with lips and tongues and fingertips.

It is anyone's guess how much the island itself transformed us. It could be that Isaiah's music, combined with the ancient artistry of the love-beads, contributed to our sea change. After I cajoled Isaiah with the *ahweniee*, and its melody penetrated his skin as deeply as his songs did mine, I asked if he felt the same as me, and he nodded. I can't explain precisely what happened or when the transformation occurred. It seemed perfectly natural. Lyin aiah's thigh. If we weren't fishing or toying with the *ahweniee*, we spent our afternoons dancing to a transistor radio: Fela, Osibisa, and Highlife— we danced to whatever was playing.

Everything was wonderful to begin with. Isaiah had brought some marijuana with him. We didn't smoke much. In fact, we barely smoked at all, because by the start of the second week, Isaiah was beginning to see and hear things.

A week after our arrival, a Tuesday, we barbequed fish and ate avocado. We'd caught the fish that morning—another taboo broken. No one's supposed to go fishing on a Tuesday. It's a day of rest for fishermen, the day when the lagoon replenishes itself. Around three in the afternoon, when the sun was beginning to sink, Isaiah pulled on a T-shirt and began rolling a joint.

I can see Isaiah now sealing two slices of wafer-thin paper with a lick of his tongue. His eyes are an intense blue-black, his skin a smooth chestnut brown. His leonine face and fluid features point to a mercurial, affectionate personality. He's a young man easily amused, often distracted. Some consider him frivolous, others the spoilt son of a privileged family. If I have learnt anything over the past week, it's that Isaiah needs me to believe in him, to have faith in his abilities.

He lights the spliff, and after a deep drag offers it to me. I barely inhale. I haven't smoked much since Isaiah started describing, in minute detail, objects he sees and insists on showing me: giant soldier ants under our cover-cloth at night, bats at rest in the orange grove. I see nothing; hear nothing. I watch over him.

"Can you hear it now?" he asks, his head cocked to one side.

Whenever he poses that question, which has been often lately, I think he's fooling around, trying to frighten me. This is what I believe, till I notice a prick of fear in his eyes; then, I know he's not kidding. He wants reassurance that we're in this together, that he's wise to whatever's encroaching on our haven. Convinced we're not alone, he wants to persuade me too. "What can you hear, Isaiah?" I reply.

He hears running feet. "She's after us," he says, a note of dread in his voice. "She's coming for us."

"Who are you talking about? We're the only ones here!"

There's someone else, Cuba. Can't you feel her?"

I shake my head and inch closer to him. I look around.

"The mistress of the shrine."

"But, Isaiah, you don't believe in that stuff, and neither do I. We're alone. You *know* we are."

105

I grab his hands and gaze into his eyes, determined to anchor him in reality. He's shaking, his pupils dilated, his brow beaded with sweat. I clasp him tightly, trying to calm him with the warmth of my body. I do everything to sooth him, but the tighter my grip, the more unreasonable he becomes. "She's coming. I hear her coming," he cries.

"Hush, Isaiah. It's all right. I'm here."

"Listen!"

For a moment, there isn't a single sound to be heard, not even the faintest waft of breeze. An eerie calm has sealed us in a cocoon. It is as if, all of a sudden, the earth itself has shivered, and in that instant every insect, beast and fowl, alert to danger, has paused to take note of an unnatural event. Then I hear a faint echo of distant thunder. A cloud covers the sun and, as the thunder recedes, shadows invade our haven, leaving it in preternatural dusk. The glade is silent, but for our stilted breathing, and I suddenly have a nagging, chilling certainty that something incomprehensible, beyond our control, is taking place.

I clutch Isaiah so fiercely that I can feel his heart racing. He's terrified too, yet his arm around me is protective as he drags me under brushwood to hide.

Bereft of noise, shrouded in light that is neither day nor night, the clearing appears to quiver. We brace ourselves against what is to come. One moment it is tranquil, uncommunicative; then, as the shadows deepen, the glade shudders with life. We hear insects first, screeching cicadas: after that, the piercing shriek of monkeys and cormorants, compounded by an insistent beating of wings, a slow, resonant drum roll of sound followed by a squall that slashes leaves off the trees and flings dust in our eyes. We are cowering in the undergrowth, submissive, our bodies huddled in the vain hope that if only we make ourselves

small enough, events will pass us by. "Don't look," Isaiah
warns.

I couldn't have looked if I'd wanted to. There was too
much debris: twigs, leaves, ash; the wind tossed everything
into the air—our home, our worldly possessions, the detritus
of a week on the island—making it impossible to distinguish
shapes or forms in the cacophony of sound and motion around
us. Even so, I felt a presence inching towards us. I sensed
something coming, and, petrified though I was, I wanted to see
it. I had to look at whatever was closing in, in order to save
myself.

Then, as suddenly as it had started, the wind dissipated,
and a cool, furtive tranquillity reigned once again. Clearing dirt
from my eyes, I peered through the undergrowth and made out
a figure at the centre of the glade. A thin shaft of light between
a pair of trees delineated her silhouette as she drifted nearer.

My first impression was of dragonflies; the wings of
dragonflies at dusk. The apparition appeared to consist of
thousands of insects in motion, and the light shining through
their wings illuminated the figure in iridescent glory. "Sweet
Jesus," Isaiah cried.

We were trespassers, trapped in a place where we didn't
belong, yet imminent danger, combined with terror, paralysed
us. Unsure what to do, I began to stand up. Better to run, I
decided, than wait to be caught. Isaiah tried to pull me down
but I dragged myself up again. As I did so, I hugged my arms to
calm my body's trembling. I could no more control the spasms
of fear that rooted me to the spot than I could the violent
beating of my heart. I was floundering, shaking. Inadvertently,
my wavering hand rubbed the *ahweniee*. My fingers, pressing
hard against it, dug it into my flesh in a futile bid to return us

to happier, more innocent days. Frozen, I could only watch as the shade drew closer. With her came an overpowering scent of flowering Neem trees; a sickly sweet perfume that, filling my nostrils, almost squeezed the breath out of me, so that for a moment I thought I would suffocate.

My senses began to riot as convulsions ripped through my body, and in that instant, I felt something foreign, from deep inside, take possession of my being. A transcendent voice I had never heard before roared from the depth of my lungs, and, filling me with rapturous sound, glided from my tongue in a crescendo that claimed ownership of the glade. It swung off the branches of the trees, and bounced off leaves and fruit; the voice whirled in a tornado of joy, till it peaked higher than the sky itself.

It was me and not me; otherworldly, yet familiar. It was powerful, vibrant, a tone threaded with a light, golden quality that, extinguishing every particle of fear within me, set my spine tingling. More surprisingly, it harmonised in a language I didn't speak or understand. And while it soared in ecstasy my feet felt shredded with thorns.

Believe me, it wasn't my voice. I can't for the life of me hold a tune. Yet the song that emerged from my mouth consumed every fibre of my being, every drop of my soul. Isaiah claimed that the longer I sang, the louder the music became, and with the voice exploding in his ears, the dragonflies fluttered away, scattering the shade, so that darting, trembling, it finally disappeared.

Once the rendition came to an end, the pain in my feet was such that I collapsed in a heap on Isaiah.

Master Class

Kerstin Norborg
Translated by B. J. Epstein

I know how I want it to sound, and this isn't it. I understand everything he says, this teacher, the master violinist. He talks about the role of silence in music, about how silence must also be performed, that emptiness too has a substance, and he illustrates what he just said with a judo movement on the floor, right in front of us and the instruments.

"If I am not able to fill this void," he says and points at the air in front of him, before the somersault, "I'll hit my head on the hard wooden floor."

The planks are wide, light, smell faintly of pine, and the first time he somersaults, he holds his left arm in a half-circle before him in order to mark the empty space, both for himself and for us. Then he somersaults again, without marking the emptiness. There is a murmur of suppressed delight among the audience.

"And in the same way that I held myself in relationship to the empty space between myself and the floor," he says, possibly a bit out of breath and with his tie thrown back by the draught, "in the same way, you must relate to the silence

109

in the music you have just played. Otherwise, excuse the bad metaphor, the music will also fall flat to the ground."

He quickly touches his forehead, as though he has just remembered, or wants to be sure of reminding us, about what could have just happened. And suddenly I become aware of the bags I have on my feet. "Take care of our floors and use shoe covers", it said on a sign when we came into the building, so we have just played the whole E-flat major quartet wearing blue plastic bags, the kind you usually have on at the hospital. Blue shines from the audience too. Only our teacher, I now see, hasn't protected the floor. Probably because he always knew he was going to do that somersault. No matter how we played, he'd planned to talk about silence and emptiness, and then to illustrate it with his body.

His English has an Oxford accent and makes me think of that English NATO general who announced the bombing of Belgrade. A self-assured, well-bred, almost discreet tone. And yet with an unquestionable authority. It is Mozart's E-flat major quartet we've just played; I'm second violin. I love the way we start in unison and how the voices then separate, as though anxious. And I want this sense of anxiety to permeate the whole piece, as well as the silence he's talking about; I understand and sympathise with what he's saying, with the emptiness, the air around the music.

But I can't. When I hear his words, I feel exhaustion and heaviness come creeping into me. This inability slowly spreads out into my arms and legs, into my fingertips and toes.

"Can you describe what you just played?" the teacher says, and his voice is light and humorous. Without saying anything funny, there is a freeing distance between his words and his tone of voice. It is that emptiness, I think, something he places between himself and what he says, so that the words don't fall flat onto the ground, or maybe they stick to his skin. But how can you reach that distance? My body has been transformed into a motionless mass and somewhere inside of it hides something that longs for the coolness of the music, for those vertiginous racing sixteenths that suddenly break free and live independently of me and the heaviness. Now he asks us to start playing again.

"Just the beginning," he says, and then adds a few words about what I was just thinking, about the unison and the anxiety that is there from the jump in octave in the first bar and that then escalates when the voices separate.

And I think: how can you play this anxiety and yet keep it away from yourself? How can you touch the anxiety without being swallowed up by it?

This, I think, is the difference between me and this master violinist; that he manages to bring in the air that makes it possible. And I feel the heaviness, how it grows in my body.

We begin to play and I try to concentrate on lightness. I think in long phrases, try to see pictures of deserted beaches and bare white rooms, feel the taste of lemon and mineral water, but this requires such effort that it also estranges me from the music. And instead another picture forces itself into my head. It bothers me, I try to push it away, and now this is taking all my concentration. And yet it doesn't work. No matter how hard I try, she looks out, the fat woman I saw on Drottningtorget Square the other day, the one who with an anxious expression and greedy hands ate chips so that the ketchup ran down the corners of her mouth. She is there, places herself like a raster between me and the musical notations, her anxious greedy eyes, her smell of chips, her wobbly upper arms.

The teacher stops us and says in an appreciative voice that we have really taken on what he just said, that the anxiety, the nerve, in the music is now completely different than during the first run-through, that his gymnastic exercises (yes, he really says that and he says it as though with quotation marks around the words) seem to have created results, that we now relate to the emptiness.

Doesn't he hear the heaviness? Doesn't he feel the seriousness that sludges into the tones? I peek at the others. Paula looks pleased behind her cello, as happy and clear as though she had just done that somersault. Even Tobias seems satisfied, but then he always is, annoyingly unmoved by his playing, as though it was always someone else who did it for him. Mia, I think, is as heavy as I am. But that's in the nature of the viola, that slightly trapped, veiled tone.

Now the teacher takes his violin out of its case; he wants to show Tobias a phrase in the first violin's part. And his playing is like his talking: light, brilliant, as though unmoved, but also very musical. I find myself wishing it weren't the case, wishing that his playing was just technical, a little boring. But on the contrary, it's sensitive. And his tone, it is almost supernaturally beautiful, shimmering, like lips on an eyelid. He has a balanced vibrato, and he shapes the tones both with that and the bow, searching through the phrases. No, I really can't find anything to fault. And still I want to find a fault? Now I look at the plastic shoe covers again, how blue they glow out there in the audience and on us four on the podium. Just not on his shiny black shoes. And suddenly I see how ridiculous he is, how ridiculous the whole situation is: the audience's devotion, our benevolent openness, his shiny polished words and practiced movements and all that glowing blueness. In my heaviness, there is also

112

a rage, and it is fed by his shimmering tone. Yes, I know now that if this man doesn't stop playing soon, I will have to get up and leave the room, otherwise I will start screaming, in the middle of Mozart's music. But he stops; his sense of virtuosity also seems to be well balanced. Just when he is about to go on too long, he stops himself, dries the violin, places it back in the case and nods at us, smiling, to continue.

When we start the movement from the beginning, the ketchup woman is there again; I feel her from the first bar. In her expression and movements, there is nothing of the judo movement's airiness. Everything about her is nervous, pushy, too much, it isn't possible to fight against her anymore—I let her fill my playing. Carefully, I glance at the others again. Paula is playing with her eyes half-closed, in full concentration. During the reprise, I note Tobias's look of appreciative surprise, and I hear a resistance in his tones that wasn't there before, how they almost dig down into his instrument, get a taste of its wood before they leave him, flying. I am sitting too close to Mia to see her, but I feel that we are in the same movement now, that we are being carried. Is it the ketchup woman who is carrying us, is it her we are playing? It doesn't matter anymore, I also feel the taste of wood, the friction, how the tones push against me and the instrument before they leave. The heaviness is still there, but I ignore it, play. And to my great surprise, I discover that now I am part of the music.

Agony in the Silence

Elieshi Lema

*P*amela got the news of the death of Petro and Rebecca's son in the casual way in which people talk of death these days.

"Have you heard?" the man said. "Can you believe that Rogathe, Edward's younger brother, is dead?"

"Who are you talking about?"

"I am talking about Petro's son."

"What happened to him?" Pamela asked in astonishment.

The mobile phone had brought news from the village. The news sounded like gossip, as if death was a subject of popular interest. The caller had talked of the burial and about the crowd that had turned up to pay their last respects.

"He said that many people had just gone to watch how he looked like at his death. Just that, Ma Pamela. So many people turned up just to see a dead body!"

"And what did they say he looked like?" Pamela asked.

The man answered. "The caller said that he looked normal. As if he was sleeping. This disease is very strange. It hides its face."

"What disease are you talking about?"

"I hear he died of the disease of these days, although at burial they said he died of liver failure."

"So which was it? Complications of HIV/AIDS or liver failure?" Pamela asked.

"I do not know, Ma. I don't know," the man said. "The caller said that the women did not weep, except the mother. They have given up their role of weeping and wailing. They gave up when the village started receiving two coffins a week. The caller said that these days the village is as quiet as a graveyard, Ma Pamela. The stories of death are many. Blood pressure, malaria, ulcers, and now this one has died of liver failure. Rogathe was my age mate, Ma. He was thirty-two years old when he died."

"So young!" Pamela said, engrossed in thought. She wondered if a time would come when people would get the courage to face the scourge squarely.

Rebecca, the mother of the young man, was her childhood friend. They had maintained the friendship through the years and in spite of their different lives. The memory of their earlier lives momentarily pulled her thoughts away from the news bearer before her. Then he cleared his voice. "His brother Edward brought home a daughter, about six years old or so. But even the daughter . . ." The man shook his head.

"What did the mobile phone say about the daughter?" Pamela asked, irritated by the man's tone. As he continued to shake his head, Pamela added: "I really should find time to go and give my condolences."

116

"Me too, Ma Pamela, me too. We went to school together. I should go. Maybe I should call Edward in Arusha to say how sorry I am. But about this child he brought . . . I hear the mother is on the deathbed too."

"So Rogathe was married?" Pamela asked.

"I am not sure, but I hear he had a girlfriend, though they broke up before his death. You know how town relationships can be. Too many temptations." He laughed.

Pamela smiled wryly. "So, is the child OK?" she asked.

"They say she looks weak. She has ulcers on her head and things . . ."

"Have they tested her for HIV? But you wouldn't know, would you?" Pamela asked.

"Test for HIV? Ehe! That is a tough thing to do. Even I wouldn't do it, Ma Pamela. Eh, no, no. It is curiosity that killed the cat, you know!" He shook his head.

In spite of the circumstances, Pamela laughed. "So you think the ones who go for tests are not in their right mind?"

"I just said that I wouldn't, Ma." He touched his chest with his palm twice, to drive the point home. "I will die anyway, when my time comes," the man concluded. "You know, I have to go," he said, looking around nervously, as if he was afraid to have his words overheard.

Pamela had parted ways with Rebecca after primary school and had gone on to secondary school and university while her friend stayed back in the village. Time pushed them in opposite directions, but their friendship survived. Pamela got married and became the owner of a private teacher's college, while Rebecca became a housewife. When they met every two or three years, it was Rebecca who would be laughing heartily, full of life, talking about her farms and crops and animals, about the bulls that she would sell off and the cows that were about to calf. She talked endearingly about her aging mother- and father-in-law, about how they needed her support. On the sitting-room wall in Rebecca's house hung framed portraits of her husband in a smart black suit, taken in a photo studio in Nairobi. There were also photos of her wedding and of her sons at their confirmation. These were her men, and their images were always with Pamela.

Rebecca had bloomed. Being a housewife had not been difficult. Her husband, Petro, lived and worked in Nairobi as a stonemason. He came home to visit his family once a year, at Christmas holidays. That was her life and she enjoyed it. But life is like that, Pamela thought. It can stretch in front of you, looking taut and full of strength and promise, and then, *snap!* without warning it recoils and hits you in the face, hard.

#

When Pamela got home, her husband had not yet arrived. She set about preparing dinner. Her children were grown and had moved away from home. Pamela preferred to prepare the last meal of the day. Her house girl was not resident in the house. Often, after dinner, Pamela would sit at her desk and work on her old laptop. She would write her teaching notes, or read, or grade schoolwork. But today she was distracted. Her mind refused to concentrate. She was happy when her husband arrived.

"How was your day?" she asked him from the desk.

"The normal routine," he replied casually. "I have spent the whole day responding to what the press said about the ministry. Then it was meetings and more meetings. The year will end before I get anything done."

He sat down on the couch and switched on the TV, then stood up and followed his wife into the kitchen. "How does that fridge look like?"

"Three Kilimanjaro beers, ice cold," Pamela said.

"I cannot stand ice-cold beers," he said. He took out two beers and placed them on the dining table to thaw. He went back into the sitting room and watched the dull soap opera on TV for some moments. Then he changed the channel.

Pamela returned to the sitting room, sat next to him.

"I got some bad news today," she started. "My friend's son died. Rebecca's son, Rogathe."

"Oh, *pole.*"

"But that is not all. He died of AIDS, although the man who told me the news said something about liver failure."

"Of course."

"Of course what?"

"Of course there is always a disease that one dies of. Remember our boss, Dr. Raymond Fasi? He was admitted to Muhimbili Hospital for a month. We were told it was blood pressure. The doctors informed the family about the real problem and suggested that he be cared for at home. But no, he had to be flown to India for treatment. Did he recover? He was the fourth senior officer at the ministry that we lost to the disease, but it was always another disease that got the blame."

"But is that right? Do you think we should keep hiding the truth?"

"Truth? What truth?"

"Baba Gama, are you telling me you do not know?"

"The issue of truth is irrelevant here. Pamela, please think clearly. Death is frightening, very frightening. Didn't we both go to the funeral of Dr. Fasi? Even the pastor, a man of

119

God who shouldn't be afraid of death, was willing to circle the truth! The pastor's eulogy had nothing to do with AIDS."

"Yes, but after the funeral service the people talked. They talked about Fasi's girlfriends and pointed them out in the crowd! They talked as if they expected Fasi to wake up and say 'I am sorry.'"

Baba Gama grunted. "No wonder he wanted to die far away from home!" He shook his head. "I tell you, he suffered enough right there in the ministry. I was shocked to learn that the canteen cooks isolated his plate without his knowledge. Whenever he went to the canteen, the waiter who never even noticed some of us would run to him and say: '*Mzee*, you cannot stand on a queue, you go sit down at a table, I will bring your food.' He thought it was respect."

"Why?"

"Maybe he thought they were trying to tell him that he needs to eat more! He thought they were sympathetic."

"You don't say!" Pamela said, surprised.

"And, even worse, no one sat near him. Once in a while a person or two would join him at the table and sit on the furthest chair, usually on the opposite side of the table. He always ate so fast to avoid the embarrassing silence. Towards the end he said he had too much work and he started asking the waiters to bring him lunch in his office. I tell you, after that, the whole department that ate in that canteen breathed a sigh of relief."

"Running away does not help, Baba Gama," Pamela said.

"I don't know . . . I think it does. It keeps the reality away, at least for a while. It hides the fear, I suppose."

"Fear, Baba Gama? Can you hide fear? Real fear? Like the one I imagine HIV must stir in a person's heart?"

"My dear wife, I am not a psychologist. I am just saying that people run because they are afraid. I imagine that the fear that comes with knowing that you house death in your body is beyond understanding when you are affected. You walk with it. When you put one's head down to rest at night, it lies down with you!"

"It must be terrible. The fear remains inside you and corrodes your soul like acid," Pamela said quietly, as if talking to herself.

Baba Gama responded with a nod and turned his attention to the TV, searching for a news channel.

"Baba Gama, do you think . . ."

"Please, Mama, I am tired, you know," he complained without turning to look at her, and then continued: "HIV is not a subject which induces rest in a man who has been working the whole day."

Finally he found Aljazeera. He walked over to the dining table and poured himself a glass of beer, then settled into the couch in the sitting room to watch the news.

Pamela thought about bringing Rebecca's granddaughter to the house to care for her. As she prepared dinner, she thought about it some more. She decided she would give her friend whatever help she needed.

Just then Baba Gama called out to her. "Is there something you wanted to ask me?"

"Well . . . I have not told you yet," she said, happy that he had asked. "Rogathe had a daughter. I hear she is not well. So I was wondering if we could help my friend out by caring for the little girl." She felt a wave of relief after she finished talking.

Her husband was silent. After a while, he stood up, emptied the beer bottle into his glass, and then said, "I don't understand you women."

"What I just said could have come from the mouth of a man," Pamela said. She stood up and strode into the kitchen. The food was ready, but still she lifted the lid and looked into the pan, then put the lid back on. She went back into the sitting room, resolving to first accomplish the task she had started.

"Why would you do that?" her husband asked when she appeared.

"I want to help my friend. If the child is sick, as I suspect she is, then she will need a lot of care. I just thought I could be of help."

"Has she asked you to help her?"

"No. She may not ask, but I know she needs help."

"You are being impulsive, you are not thinking. What do you know about care for HIV-infected children? This home is not a hospital and you are not a doctor. Oh yes, I know something else . . ." He turned to look at her. "Once you have brought the poor child here, you won't have time for her, and so, of course, the house girl will become the nurse. And, of course, it will not matter much if she too gets infected."

"Thousands of people all over the world caring for their sick are not doctors. Their homes are not hospitals, and yet they are doing it." Anger crept into her voice. She stood straight, her arms akimbo.

"What are you trying to prove?" Baba Gama said. His voice was flat, like a soda without fizz.

"Nothing," she said. She lowered her hands and sat down.

"Why don't you start an orphanage for such children? Orphanages are good projects these days, especially for women. Go on, you have money, don't you? You are forever complaining about what the government has failed to do. Now is your chance to show them how caring and considerate you are!"

"Baba Gama, don't you care at all?" Her voice was tired.

"I care about me!" Baba Gama shouted. He gulped beer and stared at the TV. Then he touched his chest with his middle finger. "And I say that without apology. I am not one of those who pretend to be Mother Theresa!"

The discussion was going nowhere. Pamela decided to wait until she met with Rebecca.

The couple ate their dinner in silence. Pamela wished her children were around, although she could not be sure which side they would take. Not that it mattered; her mind was made up. After dinner, she and her husband went to their bedroom and climbed into bed, each facing opposite walls. Just before Pamela fell asleep, she heard her husband say, "I will move out if you bring that girl into this house." She did not respond.

#

A month passed before Pamela went to visit her friend. She had, by then, worked herself into a permanent state of guilt and concern. Hers was not a Christmas visit when friends brought gifts befitting the season. What should I take to a friend who is bereaved? Pamela asked herself, racking her brain. Should I give her money or a *khanga* like most women do? Should I take vitamins for the little girl? How will I explain the vitamins? Pamela agonized for days, and then finally asked her husband.

123

"What do you think I should take to my friend?"

"What do women usually give each other?" he growled in reply.

"I am not just any woman to her."

"I would say just go and see her first and then you can decide."

"Thank you," Pamela said, but went on to do some shopping. She filled her basket with rice, tea leaves, cooking oil and sugar. She also took fruits and biscuits for the girl. A respectable woman could not go to a bereaved friend's house with empty hands, she thought.

When Pamela arrived at Rebecca's house, she found her friend sitting on a low stool in the front yard, sifting through beans to be cooked. A young girl — the poor sick child, Pamela thought — was lying on a mat close to her feet. Rebecca sprang up from the stool, agile and excited, and ran to meet her.

"Such a long time..." Rebecca exclaimed.

Pamela placed her basket on the ground and the two friends embraced. Rebecca began to weep and shake with convulsions. Pamela let her cry. She held her tightly as silent sobs racked her frame. The girl sat up on the mat and watched her grandmother and Pamela curiously.

Rebecca finally broke apart from her friend and found her voice, at the same time wiping her nose with a corner of the *khanga* around her waist. "Welcome, welcome my friend," she said, and offered Pamela a seat. Pamela picked up the little girl and perched her on her lap. She felt so light in her hands. "How are you, little beautiful girl?" she asked her.

The girl looked at her with big, clear eyes and remained silent. She gazed curiously at the guest, taking her time to study her.

Pamela, smiling at her, said, "Do not worry . . . you will greet me when you are ready. Can you tell me your name?"

The girl glanced at her grandmother as though seeking permission.

"Go ahead, tell her your name," Rebecca said.

"Patti," the girl said in a low, breathless voice.

"Patti. Patricia? I am so glad to know you. I am called Mama Gama. Gama is a big man now. He goes to college. He has a younger brother and sister."

This information was of no interest to Patti. She climbed down from Pamela's lap and walked to the basket on the ground. Pamela reached for the basket and dug her hand inside. She brought out a small paper bag containing two boxes of biscuits and some bags of potato crisps. She gave them to Patti, and then handed the basket to Rebecca.

"I was not sure what to bring for Patti," she said.

"What you brought is what she likes the most," Rebecca responded. She turned to Patti and told her to thank Pamela.

"Thank you, Grandma," Patti said instead.

"It's alright. Go on and enjoy," Pamela said.

When Rebecca entered the hut to make tea, Pamela tried to talk to Patti.

"What class are you in, Patti?"

Patti shrugged her shoulders. "*Hamna.*" Her voice was thin but firm.

"You have not started school yet?"

Patti nodded.

"When is your mama coming to see you?"

Patti ran into the hut. Pamela regretted her curiosity. Then Rebecca came out with a thermos flask and a stool, with Patti close behind her. Petro also emerged from the doorway.

125

"Welcome, Mama Gama," he said, as they shook hands.

"Thank you. I am already feeling at home."

They drank the tea in silence. After a short while, Pamela said, "*Poleni sana*. My family and I are so sorry about your son."

"It is God's work," Petro said.

"That is how it is," Rebecca said.

"What happened to him? He died so young!" Pamela's face was creased into worry lines.

"We don't know what happened," Petro said. "He was very sick when he came here. His brother Edward brought him home with the little girl."

"Oh?" Pamela said. "But didn't Edward explain what had befallen his brother?"

Rebecca was silent. She stared into her empty cup.

Petro spoke. "He just said that he was very sick. He said his daughter had no one to care for her, so he brought both of them home. Rogathe let his brother talk for him. He never looked us in the eye. When I tried to talk to him after his brother had left, he looked away and asked us to forgive him and pray for him." 'What should we forgive you for?' I asked him. My heart was beating hard in my chest. I felt short of breath. 'What do you want us to forgive you for?' I asked again. But he turned his head to the wall and tears just rolled down his face. He did not say a word."

Rebecca collected the cups as if she was in a hurry to go somewhere. She put her cup and Petro's on the tray. They had drunk their tea quickly, like villagers do. The track of warmth it makes all the way to the stomach combats the cold and is good for the organs, they said.

126

Pamela's cup was still clutched in her hands. Her tea grew cold. As Rebecca took the cups and thermos flask into the hut, Pamela sipped the tepid tea slowly. She felt that it would be rude to return the cup with tea in it.

Petro glanced in the direction of the hut and quickly turned back to Pamela. Bending forward, he said in a low tone, "She cries at the night. She started a few days after Rogathe came home. I thought she would get used to the situation, or that she would stop after his death, but no. In the morning her pillow is always wet. I don't know what is still eating her. I do not ask her, I just let her cry. But it is a very hard thing to bear."

He shook his head side to side and sighed. After some moments of silence, he added, "Please help me and talk to her, Ma Pamela."

Pamela nodded.

"Now I will let the two of you talk," he said, getting up.

"Oh, please stay. It would be nice to talk to both of you," Pamela said.

"I am going to the river to cut grass for our two cows. If I stay any longer it will get too dark for me to see. My wife used to fetch the grass, but now she has to care for the little girl."

"Yes, I can see you have no other help," Pamela said.

"Who will come here now?" He had lowered his tone again, and Pamela listened attentively. "Her friends have stopped coming to help. One by one they started saying they did not have the time. It has been hard for her. I think it was God's plan that Rogathe did not live long after he came home . . . a little less than a month and he was gone."

127

"People are too busy these days." Pamela said.

"I hear you, I hear you," Petro responded, then changed the topic. "How is your family in Mwanza?" He did not look at Pamela; he stared down at the dust with his brow creased. The lines beside his mouth deepened. Their conversation followed the pattern of a ball hitting a boulder and bouncing off, only to bump against another boulder again.

When Rebecca came out of the hut, Petro asked her to give him the sickle and the strings.

"You cannot go to the river at this time," she said.

"What do you suggest I do?"

"Look for one or two banana plants that the cows can eat this evening. Tomorrow you will go to the river."

Petro hesitated, then said: "What shall we eat after we have fed all the banana plants to the cows?"

"Petro, it will soon be dark!"

Pamela listened to them in silence for some moments. Then she interrupted. "Perhaps you could buy grass for the cows? Could some of the young girls in the village cut grass and sell it to you?"

"I no longer have work," Petro said quickly. "I came back to the village when work became hard to get in Nairobi. In the 60s I was young and strong and work was plenty. In the 80s, younger men started vying for the same jobs, but there was still work. But by the late 90s young masons from vocational schools were graduating in the hundreds, and they were stronger, more competitive. I could not cope."

"You cannot forbid God when He wants to slap your face . . . truly." Rebecca was staring at her husband as she said this. "First, Petro came back to stay here in the village. For days

128

I asked God, 'Why did you bring this man to sit with me here in this dust? And do you know how God answered? He brought me Rogathe . . . and Patti."

Petro pulled out Rebecca's stool and asked her to sit.

"It is not God, Rebecca, it is the way things sometimes happen," Pamela said. "People become sick and die and people also lose jobs. We just have to struggle on."

Rebecca glanced at Pamela with hurt in her eyes. She pursed her lips and looked away.

"It is his brother, Edward, who behaved so strangely. I told him that we needed money, but . . ." Petro shook his head. "How could he just leave us here with this child and go away? He just said that he too was struggling."

"Did he say he was sick too or that he had no money?" Pamela asked, trying to hide her fear.

"Let us not burden you with our woes," Rebecca interjected.

Pamela decided this was the moment to voice her secret wish.

"Would you mind if I took Patti with me to Mwanza?"

"To do what with her?" Rebecca's tone was sharp. Her eyes narrowed, grew misty.

Pamela was taken aback. She hesitated before saying: "Maybe the doctors could examine her to find out what is ailing her."

Silence sat between them, held their breath in its grip.

Pamela broke the spell. "There are drugs these days. People with HIV can take medicines that help them live long and healthy lives."

It was bait. Yet the silence deepened between them. Petro fidgeted on the chair.

Rebecca finally spoke. She said in a scolding tone: "Darkness is coming. Petro, leave that chair and go look for fodder for the cows. If you wait too long you may not be able to identify the bananas to cut." Petro did not move.

Rebecca reached for the beans she had been sifting and started to sort them. In no time the *ungo* with the beans sat on her lap, and her hands lay limp on the beans.

Pamela looked at both of them and knew that she could not let this situation continue. She knew she could be pushing them too far, but she asked, "Did Rogathe die of AIDS? Did he ever say what ailed him?"

"My wife has gone through enough pain, Mama Gama. Please do not reopen her wounds, I beg of you." Pamela could see the desperation in Petro's eyes as he spoke. She stared at him, trying to appeal to him with her eyes. Petro avoided eye contact. He sighed and sat back on his stool.

"Why does it matter now how he died?" Rebecca asked in such a low voice that Pamela could hardly hear her.

"Rebecca, my dear friend, you all put yourselves at risk through the care you were providing. Also, the child could be sick. It is important that you recognize that."

"What do you mean? You mean . . ." Petro stammered, but Rebecca cut him off.

"My son would not lie to me. He died of liver failure. He was in no position to lie to his own mother."

Petro tried again. "Are you telling us that Rogathe had AIDS? Is that what you are saying, just like the rest of them who came to look at him like he was an animal in the zoo?" His face contorted, he seemed ready to weep.

"Forgive me, I did not mean to hurt you," Pamela said.

"Then I beg you to stop talking about things you know nothing about," Rebecca said. She put the *ungo* down and stood up, then went to look for a *panga*, which she handed to Petro. He walked into the grove without a word. He looked like he had aged since Pamela arrived. His step was uncertain, his shoulders were hunched, he seemed about to fall on his face.

Rebecca sat down and picked up the *ungo* of beans again. Her hands worked quickly, feverishly sorting the beans. She stood up and put some water in a pan, pouring it from a big barrel that stood beside the hut's entrance. She put the beans in the pan and went into the hut, taking the pan with her. When she came out her eyes were red from blowing the wood fire.

She sat on her stool and wiped her eyes with the corner of her *khanga*. Then she asked, calmly now: "What do you know about my son?"

"What do I know?" Pamela was thrown of balance by the question.

"Yes. What do you know about his illness or anything else?" her friend said. Her tone was hard.

"I am sorry," Pamela said. "I do not know anything about your son except what I was told. That he died of liver failure, but also that he could have died of AIDS. I am sorry . . . I am just concerned about you, my friend."

"You are not concerned. You are just curious like the rest of them. You have not lost a child who was already a man. You have not raised a child and then see the grown man brought to you like a child again. What do you know of that, Pamela?"

Pamela kept quiet. She could not pretend to know how the shoes on someone else's feet pinched. A voice in her mind warned her not to intellectualize this discussion. So she kept

131

quiet and hoped that Rebecca would talk, hoped that Rebecca would uncover her bleeding heart.

In that silence, Patti, who had trailed her grandfather into the grove, came back carrying a small bunch of bananas. Pamela had, as a young girl in the village, fed goats and calves the same green bananas, especially when the tree was uprooted by strong winds or its roots were eaten up by disease.

"Grandma, Grandpa said to ask you if you can cook this," Patti said, handing her grandmother the bunch. Rebecca looked at the bananas and said, "There is nothing to peel here. Go and tell him not to cut the banana tree down. If it has fallen, tell him to leave it as it is. It may still mature." The girl ran back into the grove.

Rebecca looked at Pamela and said, "We are competing with the cows now." And she laughed drily.

After a while, Rebecca sighed and said, "God gave me a hard test and I survived it, Pamela. But I asked him, why me? He did not respond. God kept quiet. And in the time my son was dying in bed, two coffins were brought to the village. I went to bury one of them, but I did not go again . . ." She shook her head.

"Why?" Pamela asked in a whisper.

"I heard words that chained my feet to this home. The words pricked my heart like thorns. If I did not know those men and women, if I had not sat with some of them in church and sung from the same hymnbook, I would have said they were heathen, that they did not know God." Her eyes filled up, but she continued talking as the tears flowed down her face. "If I had not seen their children grow up in this village, I would say they were childless."

Rebecca wiped her eyes. When she looked at Pamela, her eyes were empty of expression, as if her soul had left her body or had sunk into some unreachable place. Pamela felt pity tug at her heart. What suffering, she thought. "I understood," Rebecca continued. "I understood why God went silent on me. I was not the only woman who had lost a grown child. But what I could not understand was why people talked like that about the death and pain of others . . ."

As Pamela listened, the scene with her own husband crept into her mind.

"When they were lowering the body into the ground, a woman standing beside me said, 'Yes, let him be buried with his sins.' I turned to look at her and said, 'Does death come only to sinners?' She looked at me with such scorn! She pursed her lips and drew her *khanga* tighter around her shoulders. She turned away as if my mouth smelled foul. As if it emitted a disease that could reach her through the air. She turned and went away from me, carelessly stepping on the stones which marked out the graves. I will never forget that woman's look. I headed home as they were singing the last hymn just so that I could walk alone. My shoulders ached as if I was carrying a huge load. When I arrived home, I could not look at my son. He heard me come back, but I did not go into the room to greet him like I always did. That evening I could not feed him. I asked his father to clean him and give him his supper."

"I am sorry," Pamela said.

"When I saw him in the morning, he was sitting up in bed, he was smiling. Imagine, *he* was the one trying to cheer me up." She paused and stared into the night—it was like she was looking at her son as he sat up in bed. Then she continued. "He asked me to put a chair outside for him so that he could bask

133

in the sun. I looked into his eyes and death looked back at me. I could not smile back as I always did with him. I could not say those words of encouragement which came to me whenever I saw him smiling or acting strong. I knew I had lost hope for his recovery. That woman at the graveyard had taken away all my energy. Her scorn had killed my hope. It was only later, after Rogathe had died, that I realized she was the angel of death. That woman made me die while I still breathed . . .

"And she was right, you know. She was right. My son disappeared less than two weeks after that encounter, like a dry leaf blown away by the wind. God took him away, beyond the sight of these two eyes," Rebecca said, touching her eyelids with her fingertips. "I tied a cloth tightly around my waist and buried my son like the other women had buried theirs."

Rebecca inhaled sharply, and then released the air from her lungs as if it were solid and heavy.

"No, Rebecca, she was not right to behave like that. You are right: such behaviour is corrosive, it destroys those it is aimed at." Pamela continued: "She did not know it, but she was afraid. She imagined that AIDS would get her somehow . . . she was just afraid."

"Afraid? You say the woman was afraid?" Rebecca looked into Pamela's eyes. "Who was not afraid? Do you think I was not afraid? Do you think Petro was not afraid? You don't know anything, Pamela," she finished, shaking her head.

Pamela was pushed into silence again. She wondered whether she should just leave, although she still wanted to help Patti.

Rebecca interrupted her thoughts. "Edward was the one I wanted to talk to. I wanted to ask him the questions that his younger brother had denied me answers to. But Edward stayed here for just four days after burying his brother. While here, he sat with the men and I was with the women. There was no space in this house where we could sit alone and talk. Mourning is a difficult time for a woman. The pain of memories weighs her down, the loss of a child weighs her down, the thought of loneliness weighs her down, and then the weight of custom and tradition are also added to what she already bears. Perhaps that is why a woman in mourning ties her stomach, to be in touch with her loss, to keep it close to her chest so as to know that she is bound to that loss until custom allows her to move out of it and think and find herself again . . ."

"So true." Pamela paused then asked, "What questions did you want to ask Edward?"

Rebecca looked at her friend, as if to assure herself that she would not be mocked. "I wanted him to tell me what he knew about his brother's sickness. I was seeking some information that I knew I had not been told. I wanted to know where Patti's mother was. Why couldn't she care for her child? What should I tell this little girl if she asks for her mother? I wanted to know about Patti's health."

Pamela did not know what to tell her friend. She had thought she would be in a better position to know the answers to things. That she would tell Rebecca what to do, what medication to give Patti, what foods to feed her. She felt weak, useless.

She straightened her shoulders. "You need to have Patti tested for HIV," she said.

It took Rebecca some time to respond, and in that silence Pamela added: "That is when you will get the information you need."

"What information will the test give me?"

135

"The knowledge that your son could have died of liver failure, but that it was a condition of AIDS. If you go for tests, you will know if Patti is safe or not. And that will help us to care for her better."

"So, that is how it is. AIDS hides in another disease. What shall I do if Patti has this thing? What shall I do?" Rebecca was not addressing Pamela; she was not even looking at her. She glared at the night and dialogued with her fate.

Petro returned from the grove with two bunches of banana riding on his right shoulder and the *panga* swinging in his left hand. The load looked too big for his frail body. The bananas dripped sap that soaked his clothes. The old sap stains on his shirt and trousers had become patterns in the fabric. Patti walked behind her grandfather, carrying two wide leaves on her head. They put their loads on the ground by the side of the hut door.

Rebecca uttered a deep groan as Petro approached the two women. "What is the matter?" he asked.

Rebecca remembered the beans she had left boiling on the fire, and she stood up quickly. "The fire must have gone out. I will be back shortly."

She entered the hut. Petro sat down. Patti went after her grandmother, and Petro, following the girl with his eyes, said, "She has been doing that since she was left here with us. She follows us everywhere. She used to follow her grandmother even into the toilet. She would stand outside the toilet door and ask, 'Have you finished, Bibi? Bibi?' and she would keep calling until Rebecca came out." Petro eyes shone with affection. Pamela smiled.

Rebecca came out of the hut with Patti close behind her. Patti was eating a biscuit. Rebecca sat down and Patti climbed into her lap. Rebecca embraced her.

"Help me tell him," Rebecca said to Pamela.

Pamela addressed Petro in their mother tongue, which Patti did not understand. When she finished speaking, Rebecca exclaimed, "My God, we are finished. The child came to take me with him!" Her voice was very low.

"No, no, no, you are not finished!" Pamela exclaimed. "But you should all take a test to ascertain your status. And once you do, you can get drugs, ARVs as they are called."

Petro's right hand supported his chin, as if his head had suddenly become too heavy for him. He said, "Bibi and I are old. Dying is expected. But what shall we do with the little girl? We don't even know where her mother is. What shall we do?"

Pamela thought quickly. "This is how it is," she said, struggling to find the right language so that the boundaries of taboo were invaded softly. "The seed of the man and woman have no virus. Virus is in the special fluid in which the seed swims. And if the inside of the woman's private parts have no bruises or cuts, then the child can be made without being affected. So Patti has a chance. You all must test so that you can all be sure of your status. My husband and I test regularly. You never know."

As Rebecca and Petro exchanged glances, speaking to each other with their eyes, Pamela waited expectantly. The silence stretched. Pamela decided to prod them into a decision. Looking at Petro, she said, "Can we agree that the best way to go forward is to test? I can take you where I do my own tests."

Petro looked at his wife, and then nodded. Pamela knew she had scored a hit. "It would be better for Patti to have her tests done first."

Silence greeted her suggestion.

"Be bold, my friends," Pamela pleaded. "It is the only way to help her."

Rebecca made as if to speak, but her lips moved without forming words. In the skies, birds flew and cried. When Rebecca raised her face, she found Petro looking at her.

"Petro, what should we do?" she asked.

"We shall hold on to God, like we did with Rogathe's illness," Petro said. "No one will even know. If what she says about the medicines is true, then we shall manage."

Rebecca looked at Pamela and said, "I will prepare her in the morning. She will be OK, I think." She sighed deeply and pushed Patti from her lap. As Rebecca stood up to go and attend to her cooking meal, Patti walked to her grandfather and clambered into his lap.

"Thank you, my friends," Pamela said. "Whatever the results, you can count on me for support. This child is as much my grandchild as yours."

They were all exhausted by the time they went to bed.

Pamela woke up early. She had tasks at home that she had to attend to. When Rebecca insisted that she at least wait for breakfast, Pamela said, "This is my home. I have always eaten in this house. Today you can let me go without food. Besides, last night you fed me like a calf and I am still full.

"If you have decided, we shall let you go."

"And, remember, I will be back soon. You and I always have unfinished business. That is why we need each other."

The two women laughed and hugged and said their goodbyes. Before Pamela left, she took a small wad of notes from her handbag and passed it to Petro in a handshake.

"Thank you, Ma. More will come to you," Petro said. His face had brightened; a smile played on his lips.

"Do not forget to call me," Pamela said.

"We shall call you as soon as we return from hospital," Petro answered.

"All will be well, my friends. I will pray for you."

"Thank you," Petro and Rebecca said together, and Patti, a second later, imitating her grandparents, shone a smile at Pamela and said, "Thank you."

Journey to Loliondo

Ayeta Anne Wangusa

We met on a bus in Ubungo Park in Dar es Salaam. The bus carried only sick passengers. Our journey to Loliondo was to partake of Babu's *dawa*. Our eyes met when I stepped into the bus and took the seat next to hers.

Babu's fame had spread like wildfire around East Africa, courtesy of the media attention that was focused on his miracle centre in the village of Samunge in Tanzania's Loliondo district. A retired Lutheran pastor in his seventies, he charged Tanzanians 500 shillings for a miracle drink that could cure ten chronic diseases. For foreigners, he charged 1500 shillings. Some of the passengers had been plucked from the hospital beds of Ocean Road Cancer Institute and loaded onto the Loliondo-bound bus by their desperate caretakers. The stench of cancerous wounds seeped into the air and brought bile to my mouth. An emaciated AIDS sufferer with anaemic eyes and thin skin sagging off his face clasped the metal backrest of the seat in front of him. The bus swung right and left to avoid potholes caused by the prolonged rainfall in the month of May.

The conductor walked down the aisle of the bus, checking to see if we all had bus tickets while reassuring us that we would not spend more than three nights in the queue that awaited Babu's *dawa*. It was 6 a.m. and we wanted to know when we would get to Babu's.

"The journey from Dar to Arusha will take us eight hours and from Arusha to Samunge village will take us six hours. We will get to Babu's in the dark and you will join the queue in the early morning."

There were hisses of exasperation from different points of the bus, but the conductor casually said, "You have to have patience if you want your miracle." A few voices chanted "Amen" as the conductor walked back to his seat.

The road from Dar to Arusha was top quality tarmac, thanks to Tanzania's good relations with Western countries and its World Bank-acknowledged creditworthiness. The huge traffic of vehicles to Loliondo had opened up the dusty Mto wa Mbu–Loliondo road, which until recently was avoided by motorists because of banditry. The government was yet to find a financier to tar the road. The Dutch government, the third largest investor in Tanzania, which had promised to continue support for projects like roads, could no longer be relied on. This was because the global financial crisis had forced Western countries to cut their budgetary support for developing countries, causing many African countries to seek new friends from the Far East.

Loliondo district, which is in the heart of Tanzania's northern circuit wilderness, had suddenly become the apple of the eye of politicians, businessmen, and also ordinary folk like those hunched over with disease in this bus heading towards the miracle worker in Samunge. Perhaps one of the government ministers who had drunk Babu's *dawa* would clinch a deal with China, Brazil, India or Malaysia and get the Arusha–Loliondo road tarred.

Airtel had beaten her competitors to become the first mobile phone company to erect telephony masts on the hilltops in Loliondo. This had helped ease communication between the sick and their families back home. Apart from the buses that cut through the Serengeti wilderness, small chartered planes from Nairobi and Kampala also ferried the wealthy sick from Kenya and Uganda to the bustling village of Samunge.

#

A whooping cough startled the silence. I turned to my neighbour and our eyes locked again. The repeated cough from behind us buzzed in our ears. I reached out for the half-litre bottle of Kilimanjaro mineral water and passed it over my shoulder to the coughing man. I prayed to God that he was not a runaway TB patient from Muhimbili Referral Hospital. After a few sips of water, the coughing subsided. A sombre serenity hung over the bus, which was silent save for the hiccups that came from the emaciated man with loose skin on his face. My water was gone and I looked to my neighbour for help, hoping she had some water to spare. She shrugged her shoulders when I made my request. I couldn't bear the repeated cough from the emaciated man's throat and decided to engage my neighbour in small talk.

"I hope you don't mind me asking, but why are you going to see Babu?"

She first frowned at me, and then her face cracked into a smile. "For Babu's *dawa*!" she exclaimed, as though to say: "Hallo, dummy, isn't it obvious?"

I knew I appeared too forward. I hadn't planned to make her uncomfortable; after all, it was obvious that everyone on the bus was sick and needed to see Babu urgently. But I asked more questions, hoping to start a conversation and stop the sharp sound of the coughing, which was grating my eardrums.

"I hear that Babu's *dawa* can treat ailments even beyond his list of ten."

"I have heard so many stories about Babu's *dawa*. Some stories are about people dying before getting back to their families. I am just giving it a try. All you need is faith and 500 shillings," she said. Her face brightened and she chuckled.

"And the bus fare . . . and three nights on the road," I added.

She nodded, then loosened up. "I have fibroids. Terrible bleeding every month. I am hoping Babu's *dawa* is the answer. Just like the woman in the Bible who bled for 12 years, I hope I will be able to touch Babu and get my healing." She laughed softly.

"I hear you, my sister," I said. "I'm also hoping Babu's *dawa* will heal my sciatica pain. I have had pain in my right leg for the last ten years. All the doctors I have visited seem to have got richer but left me sicker!"

At my rejoinder, she thawed and opened up. We soon forgot about the coughing man behind us and exchanged stories about the many healings attributed to Babu.

#

I told her about how I found myself at the entrance of the China Modern Hospital in the dusty suburbs of Dar. An advert had broken the monologue of the ITV eight o'clock evening news on my TV screen, announcing the new hospital in town that combined alternative and modern medicine from China. The

144

hospital, a yellow concrete building, was the direct result of the long handshake of friendship between the People's Republic of China and the United Republic of Tanzania. Blood-red symbols of the Chinese alphabet dripped off the yellow wall, announcing: *Hello Tanzania. China Welcomes You.* As the TV commercial ran, a voice in Kiswahili played alongside the image of a male nurse, face turned away from the camera, tapping the back of a crying baby. *Free malaria treatment for mothers and children . . . come to the hospital for free modern malaria treatment,* the voice sang. *Are you suffering from endless pains that have no cure? Come to China Modern Hospital and meet our experienced acupuncturists . . .*

I was welcomed to the hospital by a young Tanzanian receptionist seated in a glass cubicle. Her greeting squeezed through a hole in the glass. I returned her greeting. She asked me who I wanted to see and I explained my ailment. I paid the consultation fee, which was subsidized. She gave me a receipt and a file and pointed out the direction to the doctor's room. I joined the queue on a bench outside the doctor's door. It did not take long before a male nurse approached me and asked about my ailment. I explained my condition and he asked me to enter the room after the patient he was attending to had left. He rushed off to another cubicle after his name was called. The patient who was with my doctor soon came out, and I peeked into the room to announce my presence. The Chinese doctor waved me in and pointed at the seat behind his desk.

I greeted the doctor in English and he had responded curtly in the same language before yelling the name of the male nurse who had spoken to me earlier. I was perplexed as to why the doctor appeared uncomfortable in my presence. Suddenly, he called out desperately: *"Haraka, haraka, Njoo hapa,* Masanja!" and then turned to me and calmly asked me to wait. *"Subiri."*

145

I later learned that the Chinese doctor could not speak English and the male nurse was not a nurse but his translator.

#

It was a coincidence: she had also been to the same hospital! She had learnt about the new hospital on Clouds FM as she drove to work. The advert was aimed at women with uterine fibroids, and it advised them to seek out an alternative remedy at the new China Modern Hospital in Dar es Salaam. During her lunch break she had rushed to the dusty suburb where the hospital was located. She had gone through the same routine of registration that I had, and was ushered to the door of the Chinese gynaecologist. When her turn came, there was a quick exchange of greetings before the doctor called out impatiently to Masanja. "*Subiri*," the doctor said, as they waited for Masanja to emerge from one of the other cubicles. Her doctor busied himself by doodling on his prescription notepad.

She later found out that Masanja had been a petty trader in Taiwan in the mid-90s who acquired a liking for Mandarin. After he learnt the language, it offered him a career as Kiswahili/Mandarin translator, especially after his clothes business collapsed. Hiring Masanja was a smart move by his Chinese employers, because he could speak but couldn't read Mandarin. Masanja would therefore never learn the tricks of the trade, which stopped him from ever progressing into an astute competitor by opening up a pharmacy specializing in Chinese traditional therapy. Instead, he became the pawn in the game between Chinese doctor and Tanzanian patient.

When he arrived at the doctor's cubicle, Masanja looked exhausted. His colleague, Wambura, had not shown up for work that day because of the low pay.

146

The doctor's small eyes focused on the notepad in front of him, as he made notes of his interpretation of Masanja's translation.

In the end, the doctor sent her upstairs to the ultrasound room. The radiologist was a short thin Chinese man, who when she strode in was standing on the balcony, looking down into the yard. When she presented him the sheet of paper with Chinese symbols, he asked her to fill her bladder with one litre of water. After fifteen minutes, the radiologist opened his door and asked if she was ready. "*Tayari?*" She nodded; he summoned her into her darkroom. There was no nurse in the room, just the two of them. She dropped her skirt and lowered her panties. He applied the lubricating jelly on her belly and slid the probe over her abdomen as he watched the monitor of the old ultrasound machine. He was done in five minutes, and asked her to wait for his report. The report was ready fifteen minutes later. She looked up at him, expecting him to tell her what he had seen, but all he could say was, "*Siyo sawa,*" before pointing at the staircase leading down to the doctor's office. She could not read the report because it was written in Chinese characters. She had to wait to get doctor's feedback through Masanja, hoping nothing would be lost in translation.

The doctor repeated the radiologist's conclusion. "*Siyo sawa.*"

The fibroids were at an advanced stage and she needed surgery to remove them, she was told "If you try having a baby, you will have an instant miscarriage. Very bad location, those fibroids," Masanja translated.

"What! Don't you have any herbal medicine to freeze them?" she asked the doctor in Kiswahili through Masanja.

The doctor shook his head. "Unfortunately, there is none,' Masanja said. "Surgery is the only way out. But we could still do a comprehensive test to check whether the rest of the reproductive organs are OK before we make conclusive decision on the next step." When Masanja stopped speaking, the doctor smiled a Chinese smile.

"No worry," he managed to say to her in English.

She agreed to the tests and they set a date for the next appointment. The doctor passed her his business card. Just before she left, a thought struck her. Her eyes met his with apprehension. Could she trust his diagnosis? She looked back at the business card that he had handed her and her hand quivered. The last three digits of his mobile phone number ended with 666.Could she be standing face to face with the devil?

#

I teased her for being superstitious, but she shrugged her shoulders. I reassured her that at least the doctor had not been in a hurry to use the surgical knife. As she nodded in approval, I remembered my meeting with the acupuncturist at China Modern Hospital. The ward was a rectangular room that contained six beds all separated by white curtains. Behind one the curtained cubicles lay an elderly Tanzanian woman who groaned when the acupuncture needles were inserted into her back. Before the curtain between our beds was drawn closed, the elderly mama saw me remove my wedge-heeled shoes as I prepared to climb into bed.

"At least you can still wear high heels . . . I don't think you are in much pain," she mocked.

I smiled at her respectfully, ignored her reprimand and closed my eyes. Then I lay on my stomach to get my share of the acupuncture needles. Needles were stuck into me from top of my spine to my heels. I found it bearable and hoped the pain would go, but by day four of this treatment, I still felt the sciatic pain in my right leg. For the next two days of the therapy, the Chinese nurse applied an electric current to the acupuncture needles, but I still did not get relief. In fact, I got upset and left, as this was similar to the therapy I had abandoned, which was administered by a physiotherapist in a backstreet clinic in Dar. And he, too, had pointed at my wedges and said they were too high.

I had visited that physiotherapist for almost two years but had not been relieved of my pain. I had stuck to him like a flea, so that when he moved location, I moved with him. I got attached to the pungent odour of the liniment he rubbed into my muscles. He regularly applied electric current and heat at the sciatica nerve points, but the pain remained stubborn. I grew older with the physiotherapist as my companion. Even though the pain did not go away after all these years, I grew to enjoy the electrical spasms that pulled at my muscles at five-second intervals.

Then, one day, I noticed the tattered TENS machine ropes that connected the electrodes to my skin when the electrical current was passed through my body. Gradually, I began to notice my surroundings, to observe the filthy grey curtains that separated me from the crying toddler who had been born with stiff muscles and could not walk. Every day the toddler's mother, a Zanzibari woman draped in a black *hijab*, delivered the child to the TENS machine. Unlike me, the child did not enjoy the shots of electricity attacking his body, and he screamed all through his treatment. He screamed even louder when the nurses rubbed liniment into his stiff muscles. I also began to notice the young, overweight Indian man who had

149

inherited a supermarket from his deceased father, and who came in every evening for his dose of the TENS machine. It was then I realised that the TENS machine was cheating me. Instead of giving health, it forced me to share the misery of the Zanzibari toddler and the overweight Indian man.

"Stop this thing!" I ordered the nurse.

She switched off the TENS machine and I ran out of the clinic and into the sun to live my life. The pain stayed with me, but there were moments when I found a good laugh. But after a few months, I could not stand the pain anymore and decided to try more advanced medical treatment in Nairobi, on a work-related conference trip to the Kenyan capital. The doctor I met was on the second floor of Splash Laboratory Building on Argwings Kodhek Road. He recommended a combination of traction and hydrotherapy. The latter was only available at Nairobi Hospital and therefore not sustainable, as I was in Nairobi for only a week. I opted for the traction treatment, which was available at a clinic next to my hotel. A strap was placed across my chest and my pelvis. The strap around my chest was fixed tight. A weight was then applied to the strap around my pelvis to pull my spine to its full length in order to relieve the pressure on my spine.

Did it work? you ask. If it did, I would not be seated in this bus with you heading to Loliondo to partake of Babu's *dawa*, would I?

#

"That sick bastard! How could he do that?"

My new companion had just told how me she had been treated by a doctor at the China Modern Hospital. She, in fact, had been the whistleblower who caused its closure.

150

She honoured the appointment date with the doctor and made payment to the pharmacy for the drugs he was to use in the procedure. Masanja had by this time been called away to translate for the other doctors and a young student nurse had taken his place. When it was time, she lay on her back with her legs bent at the knees and her feet placed in stirrups to allow the doctor proceed with his investigation. A bright light was beamed between her thighs to guide the doctor as he inserted the speculum into her vagina. The student nurse stood by watching the busy hands of the doctor. Suddenly, power went off, and the doctor could not continue. He walked out of the room, leaving the cold metallic speculum in her vagina. The student nurse told her the doctor was looking for a torch, since the hospital did not have a generator. The doctor soon returned with a bright rechargeable lamp, but, thankfully, before he resumed his investigation, the power returned. The doctor repositioned himself and continued his probing. Suddenly he stopped, made a clicking sound with his teeth, and said, *"Siyo sawa."*

"Siyo sawa?" she repeated after him, turning to the student nurse for an explanation. The student nurse did not speak Mandarin and looked confused. The doctor grew excited; he ran out of the operating room, calling for Masanja repeatedly. *"Haraka, haraka njoo hapa,* Masanja!"

Masanja came. He listened to the doctor carefully, and then turned to her to translate.

"There is a growth just above your cervix. It is not cancerous, but he cannot continue with his investigation because it is in his way."

"What does he propose?"

151

"He said he can remove the growth, but that will be an additional cost."

After she agreed to pay for the mini-surgery, Masanja left the room. The doctor did not have the equipment to carry out a trans-vaginal ultrasound, so he decided to take a snapshot of the dilated cervix with his Samsung mobile phone. "*Siyo sawa*," he said to himself repeatedly, like it was the only phrase he knew in Kiswahili. He showed her the snapshot.

Repulsed by the image on his mobile phone, she recoiled and screamed. Her screaming and the outburst that followed attracted the attention of the other Chinese doctors, who held a quick meeting outside the operating room. A decision was reached that he could not continue with the surgery. He closed the door behind him and spoke to his colleagues in Mandarin, his voice rising angrily. The he returned to the room and asked the student nurse to clean her up and send her on her way.

"That was unprofessional and repugnant!" I exclaimed.

"That devil was not at the hospital when the official from the Ministry of Health arrived to investigate my complaint. My file had been destroyed and there was no evidence that I had ever been a patient at the hospital. My prescription and receipts from the hospital's pharmacy were the only proof of Dr. Fung's existence. The hospital manager's defence was that Dr. Fung was not a member of staff. They claimed he was only a visiting doctor and had flown back to China. His one-year volunteer service to China Modern Hospital had ended and he would not be returning to Tanzania."

#

When I left the traction therapy physiotherapist in Nairobi, I boarded a KQ flight to Dar. Seated next to me was an Indian woman reading a book titled, *Combination Therapies: Stories of Healing*. Curious about the subject matter, I began small talk with her. She said she had been a patient of the author, a Tanzanian woman of Indian origin who had been relieved of her sinusitis pain. She gave me the author's phone number, which I saved on my mobile. When we touched down in Dar, I made an appointment with the Indian author, who was called Riya. Riya healed patients using a combination of acupressure, cupping, reiki, and crystal therapy. When I visited her home in the Masaki suburb, I discovered that this petite mother of two practiced reiki to help patients to deal with fear, anxiety and stress. Riya worked at home between 9 a.m. and 5 p.m., while her husband was in the city managing the family business. I learnt from Riya that all nerve points in the body are connected to the feet and hands. I felt the twitch in my hips when she applied pressure to one of my toes. She said my pain was deep-rooted. She would rub my body with oil before she began the cupping therapy. She had different sizes of copper-plated cups to represent the amount of pain in the body to release. She would light a flame with a piece of paper and drop it into the cup. The cup would consume all the oxygen and produce carbon dioxide, which, when turned over and placed on the skin, created suction. She would slide the cup along the nerve paths, which would then open the nerves and increase blood circulation. Riya placed the smallest cup in the valley between my breasts. I hissed with pain.

"You have deep-seated misery . . . I think it is from childhood," she said. Then she added: "Not to worry," and

153

beamed a motherly smile at me. "I will use crystal therapy to relax you."

She placed a crystal stone on my forehead, another between my breasts, another above my diaphragm, and the last one above my belly button.

I became a fixture in Riya's therapy room for the next three years, because her combination therapy granted me some peace of mind. The pain was so deep in my muscles that sometimes I could not even bear the cups sliding over the nerve paths of my inner legs. But I liked her stories about family and life and India. I also told her stories of Uganda, the country of my birth.

Her husband, Mr Rakesh, was an astute businessman and held a high position in the India–Tanzania Cooperation Initiative. He was a very busy man. In her husband's absence, Riya visited orphanages or made ceramic pots for sale on her balcony. Every December she and her husband went on holiday. One day, when I arrived at Riya's residence for my therapy session, I bumped into her husband, on his way out. He was all smiles..

"Mr. Rakesh, you are really in a good mood today," I teased him.

"Haven't you heard the good news?" he said in his thick Indian accent. "Apollo Hospitals, one of India's super hospitals, will open a chain of hospitals to treat heart patients here in Tanzania."

"Wow, that's great!" I exclaimed.

After Mr. Rakesh departed, Riya came over to embrace me, like she usually did whenever I entered her home.

"I want my husband to go on holiday with our son. I think the two of them need some time to bond," she told me.

"And where will *you* be going this holiday then?" I said teasingly.

"To Kanchipuram. With my elder sister. It is one of India's seven sacred cities. It is a place we have been planning to visit for a long time. This journey will bring me inner peace. It will involve praying and fasting and I hope to get back my spiritual and bodily balance," she finished in her pleasant singsong voice.

We always talked about the different people she had healed. Her patients were mostly from the white expatriate community. Her work tools were her diary, her mobile phone, her cups and stones, and her hands. She had a few African patients like me. One of them was a Tanzanian schoolgirl who was possessed by evil spirits.

"We had a session of reiki and now she is good, very alright," she told me happily.

And yet I was not healed by her combination therapy. But I kept going back because her motherly nature and warm laughter soothed my soul.

#

The eight hours on the Dar–Arusha highway and the six hours from Arusha to Loliondo were finally behind us. We were in Babu's compound and close to receiving his cup of healing. Three hours had passed since Babu started his morning of healing, which began when one of his attendants came to our bus with a tray of metallic cups that contained the *dawa*. Babu was overwhelmed by the patients who thronged his compound, and so he no longer distributed the magic herb himself. Instead, he prayed over the *dawa* just like a priest prays over the bread and wine at Holy Communion and then gives it to the altar

155

boys to distribute. We only saw Babu from a distance. All we could do was shout out greetings to him.

"*Shikamoo*, Babu," the bus passengers chanted when the old man wandered past.

Babu lifted his frail hand, waved at the bus, and responded in a shaky but strong voice: "*Marahaba wajuku wangu.*"

We were now all his grandchildren.

After every passenger had parted with 500 shillings and drank Babu's *dawa*, the bus was finally ready to return to Dar. As I prepared for the journey, I hoped the *dawa* would succeed where everything else had failed. I hoped it would heal me in spirit and body. But would my search ever end?

As if...

Hilda Twongyeirwe

The dogs wake her up. Whines. Whimpers. Snotty grunts. At first Faith tries to shut them out by shutting her mind. But the noise is persistent. It finds holes in her ears. Holes in her heart. It finds holes in places that she cannot shut. She turns. She searches for her phone from the bedside table and flips it open. It is a few minutes past 2 a.m.

She shuts her eyes tight and tries to think about things that could lull her back to sleep. She folds her legs. Her knees touch her husband. He does not feel her. She does not feel him feel her. She sticks out her right elbow into his back. It digs in a little but he remains lifeless. He is in another world. Dead to her. Dead to the dogs... More whines. More whimpers.

She thinks of prayer. A long soothing prayer. A prayer that would send the dogs scampering away. "Prayers do miracles," she says aloud. But the noise does not give her a calm moment to compose a meaningful request to God. They just whine on and on, breaking into her string of prayer. She repeats words and phrases and forgets what to say next. She just says

157

Amen, Amen Lord, and turns away from prayer and from her husband. She is awake now.

Her mind spins to a sleep game that her aunt had taught her and her siblings when they were little children. Counting sheep. Counting and visualising sheep walking up and down the hill. "By the time you count to one hundred plus sheep, sleep will have carried you along with the sheep," Aunt Janice would tell them. Faith starts by gathering the sheep. She gathers very many of them and starts counting. one, two, three, four, five, ... The dogs sneak into the picture. Six, seven, eight, nine, ... They distort the pattern. She wonders how many dogs they are. They are so noisy. They sound as if they swallowed drums... small and big drums. The noise is very disturbing. Faith turns several times trying to find a position that would lessen the noise but there is none. She is now fully awake. Nervous and hysterical like the dogs outside. She wishes she could speak the dogs' language. Then she would open the window and beg them to stop. She would tell them of her long and difficult agenda for the day. But they are dogs. Wet nose and the revolting black lips. Dogs. That's what they are.

Faith is angry at her home that does not have a fence to shut out wandering dogs. The stray dogs that have become a menace in the village. She wonders where they come from. And what they come for. It's as if dogs from all the surrounding villages congregate in Nsambya at night. Roaming roads, lanes and paths. Sniffing from one unfenced home to another. She wishes the police or the local council or any other authorities could do something about them. Maybe poison all of them. But no, poisoning might be dangerous because Puddy too could end up picking poisoned food. Faith can't bear to lose Puddy. He has been part of their family for more than two years. She treasures him, especially for their unfenced home where thieves could enter and go as they please.

She wonders how these dogs survive. They are so many. Homeless. Jobless, perhaps, unlike Puddy who keeps Faith's home safe in the night. Even during the day people fear to step into the compound unannounced. They think he can break loose and attack them. Poor, peaceful, Puddy.

The stray dogs remind Faith of the young men that play ludo at the small corner shop where the lane from her house joins the main road. It is not clear where they come from and where they go. They are mysterious like the dogs. They play ludo from sunrise to sunset. When the sun shifts and burns their faces, they shift the board and shift the small stools on which they sit. They put their backs against the sun. Sometimes they erect a big papyrus mat as a shield against the sun, to block out the sharp rays. Their foreheads glisten in small beads of sweat. Ludo is a tough task.

They are the same faces. The same anxious eyes that follow the black and white seeds on the ludo board. The eyes that shift from one seed to another. Locked in a silent battle of which seed will win. Which seed will lose. Sometimes the boys sip black tea accompanied by hot *mandazi* scooped from the sizzling pan on a charcoal stove, stationed near the shop. The shop is owned by a short stout man who shouts conversation to the inattentive men playing ludo. He talks about the murder of the motorcycle man in Mukono who was hit on the head with a metal bar, the priest who wedded a couple and impregnated the woman shortly after the wedding, how Manchester United humiliated another strong English team in the evening match, and this and that. The sizzling *mandazi* pan is owned by a small woman who does not seem to talk much other than asking the

159

men for her 500-shilling coin for the black tea and 200-shilling coin for the *mandazi*.

"I want to go home now."

"Who is stopping you?"

"Please pay."

"Of course we shall pay."

"I need to go now."

"What is wrong with you?" one of the men says as he taps her bum. She hisses and retreats a few steps away. But she does not leave. She stands and waits for her coins. The offending man dips his right hand in the hip pocket, raising one thigh off the stool. The coins are buried deep. Other men follow suit. They thrust their hands in pockets and fish out coins. The woman counts each coin and then wraps them all in a black and white-checked handkerchief. In the evening the men melt into the neighbourhood only to reappear early in the morning. Just like the dogs which melt into the neighbourhood in the morning and reappear in the evening. Both are not to be trusted, Faith thinks, as she remembers how one day the boys almost undressed a preacher. These preachers who preach to whoever they find on their way. He was a tall, fat man. His deep voice reverberated with the Gospel. He talked to the boys about salvation and about how God cared for and loved them. The boys ignored him. Their eyes remained on the ludo board. When they finally looked up and stood up, he was happy to have attracted their attention. But theirs was a different language. By the time the villagers gathered to rescue him, his Good News Bible was a buddle of small white pieces of paper and the boys were pulling at his trousers.

"Let the man go in peace."

"Next time he will not bring his full stomach to provoke hungry people."

"Leave them. Even Jesus was mocked and beaten. Who am I to expect any better?" the man said and walked away quickly without looking back.

Faith is not sure she will sleep again. The dogs howl and whine. Her husband snores. She prays to God that the dogs shut up. But they don't. She taps her husband on the cheek. He turns and snores louder. She wants to hold his nose and mouth. Instead, she taps him again. He moves his head and their lips face each other. A longing grips her. It is quickly dispelled by the stale breath of whisky and the chortle-like noise from his nose and mouth. She envies his nature; not many things disturb him. "You won't change much. So why whine?" is what he usually tells Faith.

Faith decides not to wake him after all. She gets out of bed and turns the light switch on. The room floods with yellow light. She watches her five-month-old son in his little crib in their room. He is lying on his back. Faith has tried many times to make him lie on his tummy without success. He just keeps flipping over onto his back.

"You have to change him. If he chokes in the night while sleeping on his back he can die," women tell Faith. "Sleeping on the tummy is the most comfortable position for babies." But baby Joel does not seem to agree with them. His most comfortable position is lying on the back. He takes shot breaths that resonate against the small blue and pink floral bed sheets that cover him. Faith thinks Joel will grow into a peaceful young man. Sometimes she is not sure whether it is a thought or a wish. The boy touches her deeply. It is intricate. She can't lay a hand on the depth of her feelings for her son. She

161

wonders whether mothers love the second and third children the same. Before Joel, whenever the topic of number of children came up, her husband would say he wasn't sure how many children they should have. Then one day, after Joel, he made a pronouncement; "Two is all I can manage.," "And how many can I manage?" Faith had asked him. "Or sorry. I had forgotten," he had responded and laughed in the most cynical manner. She did not need to fight back with words of sarcasm. She could act. Unless, of course, he decided on a vasectomy.

The dogs howl louder. Faith thinks about her boss and the report she is supposed to complete. If she does not have it ready for presentation at the 2 o'clock meeting, her boss will howl just like the dogs outside. "Ooooh Faith, nooooo!" That's the reason the dogs should get lost so she can catch some more sleep and wake up energetic. But they just won't stop.

Faith goes back to the bed and shakes her husband. This time she shakes him hard. He wakes up.

"Do you hear them?"

"The what?" He sits upright in bed.

"The dogs."

"What?"

"The dogs."

"Where are they?"

"Outside."

"So?"

"Don't you hear them?"

Jembe jerks his head to one side.

"I hear them. What's the problem?" He asks.

"They are making too much noise. Please chase them away."

"You want me to go out and run after dogs at this time of the night?"

"No. You can find a way of chasing them away without going out."

"Is that the reason you woke me up?"

"Yes. They won't let us sleep if they continue making that horrible noise."

"But I was asleep. Aah."

She wants to say that sleep is all he does in the night but instead she says, "I am sorry."

Jembe gets out of bed and hobbles to the window. He parts the curtains in a small slit as Faith catches up with him. She looks outside. She sees nothing. The dogs are at an angle where they can't be seen.

"It seems they are killing a person," Jembe says.

"What?"

"Don't you hear a tired grunt buried under the rumble of noise?"

"I am not sure I hear it. Let's open the window."

Jembe opens the window. The dogs keep quiet suddenly. But one of them starts again. A loooooooong howl. Persistent.

Then one small brown dog runs towards the road and looks up and down the road. She turns and runs back. Puddy is nowhere to be seen. Jembe shouts at the small dog.

"Go!"

She stops.

"Go!"

She runs back to the road.

"Go!"

She does not go.

Faith smiles at her defeated husband.

"She is stubborn," Jembe says.

"Don't you see she has a mission?"

"A dog with a mission?"

"You mean you do not see that?"

"You and your philosophies. She is just a stubborn dog."

"You think so?"

"Oh Faith!"

Suddenly, the little dog trots back to the other dogs.

"See?"

The little dog reminds Faith of armed forces at war. How they retreat and advance. Retreat and advance. She remembers the evening international news. It was a shrill voice on Al Jazeera talking about Libya; "*Gadhafi has recaptured most of the rebel controlled areas. The rebels have retreated. They have missed Brega which they have been eying for weeks. Gadhafi says he will not bow under the pressure of NATO and the rebellion against him. NATO has vowed to reinforce the rebels*". Like the little dog, they all have missions. Retreating and advancing as need arises.

Jembe closes the window.

"Let's sleep," he says.

"It's not a person."

"I don't think so," Jembe says.

"You don't think that it is not a person or that it is a person?"

"I don't think it is a person."

"Hmm."

"It's a dog. I think they are killing it."

"But why?"

It must be a strange dog that stumbled into their territory."

164

"And they kill it?"

"Yes. If it is male. There can only be one male in a dog territory, especially during the mating season. More than that, they fight."

The howling. The grunting. It only gets worse.

"It is in pain."

"Yes."

"Do you hear them? They are moving."

"Hmm. They are."

"Let's check again."

"For what? Let's sleep and leave them to fight their wars."

"But tomorrow it will be our war as we struggle to dispose of the dead dog or dead whatever from our compound."

"What do you want me to do?"

"If you throw something at them they will disband. Run away. Then perhaps whatever it is will die from elsewhere. Not in our compound." Talking of bodies reminds Faith of Bin Laden. When bodies become more of a burden than the living.

she feels that Jembe is flustered.

"I just want to jump back into bed. Not to get entangled into a stupid dog war," he said. "And what do you want me to throw at them? Do you see any stones anywhere?"

"Surely you can do something."

"What do you want me to do? I always tell you about the spirited way in which you harass things you call useless in this room. See? We can't even find a dry battery. Or an empty tin of your vaseline. Or whatever!"

"You know clutter is not the best thing to have around. So don't start that again," Faith tells him. She does not want to discuss irrelevant things at such a time of the night. And he has this habit. Recall all the things they have not agreed upon whenever a new crisis sets in.

She turns away from him and reaches for the drawer. She searches for what to use to disband the dogs. Nothing useless indeed. Her fingers touch a plastic bag. She pulls it out and quickly goes with it to the bathroom. She puts a little water into it. It forms a small ball. She holds the new tool and giggles.

"See. This will do," she tells him.

"You don't give up."

She wants to say that he can't be more right. Instead she apologises. She rubs his arm and gives him the little ball.

When Jembe opens the window again to throw the plastic bag at the dogs, he is spell bound.

"Come and see," he calls her.

"What?"

"Your dogs."

Faith is not amused that Jembe has called them her dogs, but still she joins him.

"Oh," a short sigh escapes her. She watches the dogs in silence. Jembe does not throw the plastic bag with water. He just holds it in silence.

They are three or four dogs in the night shadows. Faith does not make out the number at first. The dogs are dragging something. When it struggles, they clutch it down. They clutch viciously until it stops struggling. Then they pull it again. The security light outside eventually shows they are four dogs. They are pulling a fellow dog. They yank it one or two metres, and it struggles. They clutch it down again. One dog at the neck, another at the tail, two in the middle. Every now and again the small brown dog dashes back to the roadside. Up and down the road, she looks and saunters back to the comrades. A spy of sorts. Faith and Jembe remain at the window for a few more minutes. Faith watches the dogs drag and bully the dog on the ground. As if they are not dogs. As if it is not a dog. As if...

She thinks of dogs and humans. She thinks of power and powerlessness. She thinks of territorial wars in the North and the South. In her bedroom. The howling travels deeper through the centre of her head, of her belly, of her feet. Until she wants to dig a very deep pit and bury it there forever. She wonders whether the dogs are also disturbed and are simply trying to silence the howling dog.

"Let's sleep." It is her turn to drag Jembe back into bed.

She is not sure she can sleep though. She would need a sleeping pill perhaps. She resists the temptation to search the tin that keeps them. "It will soon be morning," she consoles herself as she snuggles closer to Jembe. She hopes that he will not start snoring too soon.

She reaches for her phone again and searches the menu. Words are forming in her mind and she wants to record them.

"What are you doing?" Jembe asks.

"Nothing."

"But you are holding the phone."

"Something small and I will be done."

"Something small in the middle of the night?"

She desperately wants him to shut up, instead, she says, "Yes, my dear."

"Can't you do it in the morning?"

She wishes she could stuff something in his mouth to silence him.

"Some things can't wait," she adds.

"Indeed some things can't wait," Jembe says as he carelessly thrusts his arm on her thin waist which she has tried very hard to put back into shape after Joel's bath.

"Please..."

"You woke me up."

"I am sorry."

"What time is it?

"Coming to 3 a.m." His belly pushes against her.

"A bad time of night to be awake."

"I already apologised."

"I have not said that you did not."

"You are complaining."

"I am sorry."

"That's better. Now sleep my darling," she says as she painfully shuts the door to herself and starts to write;

Tonight

Puddy sits in his territory.

She-dogs surround him.

Tonight it is their territory.

They rub cheeks.

They smell each other's smell.

They lock tails and move in circles.

Another dog saunters in.

As if...

They hold it down.

This is not his territory.

Tonight its end will come.

Tonight.

Toni...

168

Rhythm of the Drum

Philo Ikonya

"*T*ime flies. Are you ready yet?" Yessi asked.

"No!" Sofia replied.

"Didn't you hear the church bell? I rang it. No winged angel; I did not fly back. You are slow."

"Yes," Sofia answered. "I heard the bell even earlier, at 3 a.m. You were snoring beside me. The priest rang it. To be the wife of a bell ringer is to learn to listen to ringing bells! I could ring them myself even in my sleep."

"And you're still washing yourself? You rub your skin too clean with that stone. The never-ending glow on your legs, any good for a catechist's wife?" asked Yessi.

There was no answer. Did he expect one?

His wife Sofia was a soft and dark skinned beauty. Everyone talked about her legs. When she wore a short sleeved busuti traditional dress, you saw her shapely arms. In church on Sundays many stared at her. Her lips were special. Just right. Small like two pods of sweet beans. Sofia's jet black hair was healthy and cut short. Just perfect.

"Did you hear me? Is beauty deaf and love blind?"

"The beauty is mine. You are only associated. Love? What love? My piece of pumice does a good job. My oils do the rest. My feet and legs need constant care."

"Hmm, early mornings are for holy thoughts," said Yessi. "My body is sacred. Feet must look good and also run. Great legs are everything in a figure, as you know. The body is holy, is it not?"

"Temple. Holy, yes," answered Yessi.

"Naturally, my arms are like my mother's... and should not the wife of a catechist glow on Sundays?"

"Oh come on! Given a small chance, small like a little crack—a *mwanya*, as your grandmother in Busia says—you really can talk! She says you speak through the *mwanya* of your beauty, the gap between your two front teeth.

"Beautiful body and clothes too. I now have my sixtieth kanga, two for each year of my life."

"No wonder your kanga cloths can no longer fit on your shelves. You need a new wardrobe. You keep moving everything and looking at yourself in different mirrors. "

"Are you not in a hurry to leave and assist at mass?" Sofia asked sharply.

"Well, it is more about the priest, isn't it? I don't have to be there before 6am."

"Your breakfast is ready. You sit down and eat and then go and serve. I shall come to church to be ministered to at the last service. I know today it is Father Yaikson on duty and he will minister thrice before he is relieved. I'll come for the third mass, when he is tired."

"I shall serve at the first one, when he is energetic," said Yessi.

"Sometimes pluck up courage."

"Eheee!"

"Have the guts to get Yaikson's ear and, as he eats his precious eggs, whisper to him that we have not forgotten that it was he who outlawed the Catholic charismatic group in Nairobi. Tell him he is well-known, I mean he is revealed or a revelation, whichever suits your mind best! Go on, tell him! Don't sit in his house like a meowing cat waiting to be fed."

"Eeeh, but you! You can say horrible things even on a Sunday morning! I have no voice to oppose Fr. Yaikson. Yes, I am his cat. He told me to remind you that your name should be spelt Sophie or Sophy and that means wisdom. He added that you should speak in his favour when the women hold elections. Since you know of his goodness to us, do it. After all, he pays my salary on time so I do not have to confess to him both my sins and my naked poverty. He reminds you that wisdom means being good. Doing the right thing at the right time."

"Preachy you will always be! Be bold. Tell him to go dictate in Nairobi. This is Namugongo, the place where martyrs died for opposing a king. It is a shame that we should be reduced to nodding and wearing aprons! Tell him to spare his messages for sermons. Dictator! I am Sofia! This is the name I like and so it shall remain. I would not change my name for his."

Yessi fell silent. He ate and drank quietly. He was cut inside his heart. He wanted to express his hurt in his own language, his mother tongue, but in his shock, he could not even recall what to say.

"All power is from God. All strength," Yessi said as he tried to pray. Yessi was also Fr. Yaikson's cook. He shopped for the parish pantry on Saturdays and accounted for every

171

expenditure. Twelve healthy eggs. That was the most important item the priest wanted. Eggs that were fresh and not halfway to hatching. Sometimes people donated eggs as church offerings but some of the eggs were found to be smelly. Father reminded his flock every Sunday that he liked his eggs fresh. "Do not bring me your rotten eggs! When I want chicken, I eat chicken," he often shouted during the sermon. Yessi could now hear him in his mind.

There were still many clothes in the wardrobe so Yessi did not notice that his wife had packed a suitcase. The sutikesi leaned behind the door against a solid block of stone, kept there in case thieves attacked at night. The sutikesi was ready for a hand to take it anywhere. If Yessi had seen it, he would have realised hell was about to break loose. He knew his wife: she was not predictable. She could pack to leave and kiss him at the same time.

Enthralled by the words of the morning psalm he had read while waiting to ring the 5am bell, Yessi tried to ignore his wife. He picked up his grey cardigan and walked to church as he listened to the echo of the psalm ring in his mind. You have searched my soul in the night. You have tried me by fire and found no malice in me. It was David's prayer for rescue from persecutors: Psalm 17, verse 3. When Yessi got to church, he did not notice two little children sitting almost naked and playing in the mud outside the church. He was truly listening to the Lord.

In the church, warmth and song filled the air. The priest entered in and walked down the aisle like a new bride. Today the frills of his clothing were so lovely and thick and flowed in neat folds over his ankles. He came in guarded by two altar boys and a small army of little girls who looked like flower girls at a wedding celebration. Tunakushukuru! We thank you! The choir sung.

Yessi could feel the air as the priest passed by. It was pure, tinted with a familiar fusion of incense. It felt clean and healthy. The girls danced and swayed left and right. It was as if their souls flew. They threw their little arms up in honour and worship. They were led by a girl called Tendi. The church was packed. The girls went down the aisle with starts and stops. They made little circles and turned out and in. The drums reverberated with holy language.

Back in the priest's kitchen, Yessi picked a big black egg from a basket. The shell was dotted with white. He shook it for a moment and then raised it to his ear. Why did Fr. Yaikson love fresh eggs so much, he wondered, listening to the egg more attentively. Was it like the endless song of a sea shell? What did he expect to hear? A prophecy? Anything better than a psalm? Yessi's nose widened, trying to anticipate a smell. He was trying to see something deeper now that the egg was in front of his eyes. He felt it with the tip of his tongue, before holding it for a while between his fingers. He felt it with the whole palm of his hand. His fingers slithered around it.

Yessi raised a teaspoon to crack the shell. He knew that Fr. Yaikson preferred that he broke the shell on the edge of the cooker even if the hot-plate was already red with heat. He looked keenly onto the hot-plate, watched the black turning red. Red fire. The shining deep red heat ate away the black colour. With the teaspoon, he hit the egg gently in the middle and held the two shells apart. Soft orange yolk and white of egg fell into a white bowl. Immediately, he began to beat it with a folk. He thought of how he would have pierced the eyes of a snake if he had seen one so black and with white dots.

Now the oil on the pan was almost smoking. He poured the thick egg yolk over it. It was flat for a while then bubbled up on the edges. Parts of the middle rose and fell too. He began to roll it back to the centre from the edges. The egg turned pretty. It became soft and beige. When he cooked eggs, especially the ones with a deep orange yolk, he always thought that the rising edges of the omelette were a frilly cloth. They were just like the type of cloth that his wife loved so much for her small inner clothes. It was the same as Yaikson's inner dress, soft and cream, a light off-white, almost pale yellow.

He hummed something about beginnings in a void, in chaos and in darkness. He picked up the egg shells. In his hands they turned into a big horn. He touched and felt it. He saw its bell-like mouth. He should have shouted out something but he did not. He just hummed his memory verse. You have tried me by fire... but find no malice in me. He did not know why, but after gulping down his cup of hot masala tea, he remembered a line from Psalm 50. He chanted: ...rebuild the walls of Jerusalem, then you will be pleased with the proper sacrifice. He did not stop to think where Jerusalem was, and why the city walls had fallen.

The constant rhythm of the drums, truuum, truuum, truuuum, truuum and humming voices found their way into Fr. Yaikson's kitchen. Tunakushukuru! We thank you!

Yessi had his mouth full. The egg tasted rich and savoury. Breakfast was done. He had tricked himself that he was cooking for Father, but he had not forgotten that Yaikson could not stand cold omelettes. Was he in search of the power such legendary eggs were said to hold? He would prepare another omelette just before Fr. Yaikson finished his last Mass. The Mass continued. The altar girls were matched in size and weight. Their hearts were aflame, dancing for God.

Sofia entered the church with her sutikesi. She carefully placed it under the bench in front of her. No one looked up. People were known to bring big offerings to church. One of her kangas that carried a warning for one to look out for wandering lovers was tied around the sutikesi and knotted to cover it and preserve it from dust. As she knelt down, she thought about the many times Fr. Yaikson had appeared at odd hours in their house when she was alone. The many times he had demanded to be served pepper hot meals. Sofia knew how to fish out the deep thoughts in her; she was in touch with herself.

She looked up and stared at the little dancing girls. She searched around their light-coloured flaring skirts. She was happy that they all wore kangas with striking messages. Mja mpe haki yake one message read. Give the servant own justice. In Sofia's language, there were no pronouns such as 'he' and 'she'. There was only 'a person'. Yet clearly a woman's place was obvious. A man's too. In the church, in spite of the little girls and boys together dancing up to the altar with the priest, adult males sat on the opposite side of females. Only children could mix. Sometimes they sat at the feet of the priest and even on his lap.

"Tunakushukuruuu! We thank you!" the song went on. Young people began whistling behind the church. With everyone else, Sophia turned to look. The Bible came as if it was flying high up in the air—floating high up above all their heads. It was carried by a pair of perfectly shaped black hands that had long U-shaped pink nails with lovely white tips. Only serving hands; the Bible was body-free. The carrier was a man and here in church men did not refuse to dress like women. He was wrapped up as if in a shroud, just like the priest. The inscription on the Bible bearer's cloth was clear to those near the isle: Jihadhari ukimwi...Beware of HIV. Messages of different types in well-blended colours were on similar cloths in every home.

Tendi, one of the young dancing girls, moved rapidly. She received the Bible from the hands of the man and gave it to the priest. The priest read from it, but the people did not understand. His ending was as usual: "This is the word of the ...."

"No, it is not," a loud woman's voice cut in like a sharp panga. The church froze. She continued, "The Lord loves courage! Not all the rulers of this world come from the God we worship. You must declare your ways! The Lord would prefer that you make public your lovers today!" It was Sofia. The people were stunned. Sofia bent down, grabbed the kanga covering her sutikesi. She ran up and covered the altar with it. Tendi jumped into the air and seemed to fly towards Sofia. But Sofia had already dressed the altar. Tendi reached out as if to close Sofia's mouth. Sofia shoved her off. It had never happened before that a shrill female voice quickly and without any hesitation answered a priest back. Sofia's voice could still be heard in all the corners of the church.

"Oh, help Lord!" someone in the congregation shouted. "Ni nini... na wewe? Ishindwe!" Evil spirit, may you be defeated! She has a demon in that sutikesi!

"If you think I am a devil, then just look at me. I say, the word of the gospel is not the end! We must be allowed to speak about it. I cannot just sit here and wait to die. I must wash my feet since nobody else will wash them, and then I must go, unless Fr. Yaikson agrees to take my sutikesi into his house and I and my husband can live with him. He is married there, my husband," Sofia said and left the church screaming.

"Take her out of here!" shouted Fr. Yaikson finally. "She is crazy!"

"What on earth is she talking about? Is she possessed?" someone asked in fright.

"Amina, Amina! Amina!" Sofia shouted back rapidly in Kiswahili.

A gap-toothed church elder, who was always silent and meditative, suddenly shouted, "We had always knelt before our Kabaka, so who are you to stand up to the priest?"

The priest nodded and grabbed Sofia's suitcase, threatening to throw it in the church pit latrine. "Huyu mama ni mwendawazimu kweli!" This woman is truly mad! Fr. Yaikson went on feigning innocence. He was determined to finish his work. His church had never been interrupted like this. Voices jostled in the singing. Souls trembled.

Fr. Yaikson held the incense vessel. The incense spewed out of the shiny silvery vessel with small gothic-like filigree figures. Worshippers bowed in deep meditation — or was it fear? A cloud of incense choked the altar area. Its thick whitish-gray colour was dense, giving Sofia the opportunity to sneak back into the church.

Sofia's eyes turned red. They were swollen and wet. She took out her white handkerchief and passed it over her sensitive eyelids. Yaikson was hardly visible. His auburn hair was standing on end. It was burning brightly. His robes turned a colourful red and yellow. His red chasuble was turning into flames too. His white alb did not have any words written on it, but Sofia was certain that she read there, 'Dawa ya moto ni moto!' and "Kazi ni kazi." She looked up again as if dizzy. Fight fire with fire! and Work is nothing but work! She rubbed her eyes again. A blur everywhere.

A new hymn began. Drums went trrruum, turrrum. Whistles blew from the back of the church. Sofia turned her head. She saw the Bible carried high above the head of a tall man in white robes as he exited the church. She remembered the Maasai moran she had seen jumping up high on TV the previous night. The rhythm of the drum invited jumps; high jumps.

Suddenly, Sofia felt she must sit down. Her stomach felt heavy, her knees weak. Her mind drifted off, woozy. In the rising incense, many things hid.

At Fr. Yaikson's house, Yessi could hear voices but he paid no attention. Another omelette sizzled in the pan. Yessi was sure the Man of God was about to come out and would need a hot egg immediately.

About the Contributors

Yaba Badoe is a Ghanaian-British documentary filmmaker and journalist. A graduate of King's College, Cambridge, she worked as a civil servant in Ghana before becoming a general trainee with the BBC. She has taught in Spain and Jamaica and is, at present, a Visiting Scholar at the Institute of African Studies at the University of Ghana. Her short stories have been published in Critical Quarterly, African Love Stories, an anthology edited by Ama Ata Aidoo, The Daily Graphic newspaper, African Sexualities: A Reader, edited by Sylvia Tamale and Pumpkin Seeds and Other Gifts, edited by Helen Moffet and Violet Barungi.

Erik Falk is a lecturer at Södertörn University, Sweden.

179

Colleen Higgs is a South African writer and publisher whose work has appeared in numerous journals and magazines. She has two poetry collections: Halfborn Woman (2004) and Lava Lamp Poems (2011). Her short stories have been published in anthologies such as Dinaane, Just Keep Breathing, Pumpkin Seeds and Home, Away, and she participated in the 2006 British Council-sponsored Crossing Borders project. While working at the Centre for the Book, Capetown, she managed the award-winning Community Publishing Project. In 2007 she started Modjaji Books, an innovative small press that publishes southern African women's writing. She is featured in the 2011 Mail and Guardian Book of Women and lives in Cape Town with her partner and daughter.

Philo Ikonya has been described as writer who claims history and creates futures passionately. She was first a school teacher and later taught Semiotics in Tangaza College and Spanish at the United States International University, (USIU) in Nairobi, Kenya. Between 2007 and 2009, when she was PEN Kenya president, she was brutally arrested several times for speaking out against corruption and the foiling of freedom of expression in her country. Born in 1959 in Kenya, Philo has lived in exile in Oslo, Norway, since 2009. She is the author of two novels: Kenya, Will You Marry Me? (Langaa, Cameroon, 2011), and Leading the Night (Twaweza Publications, Kenya, 2010). Some of her poems have been translated into German and published in a bilingual edition titled Out of Prison: Love Songs - Aus dem Gefangnis Liebesgesange (Loecker, Austria, 2010) and This Bread of Peace (Lapwing, Belfast, 2010). She has written three children's books: We Met a Grasshopper and Other Poems and The Lost Gazelle (both by East African Educational Publishers) and The Kenyan Boy who became President of America, which was translated into Norwegian: Med Røtter Fra Kenya I Det Hvite Hus (Libretto, Norway).

Mamle Kabu, a writer of Ghanaian and German parentage, was born and raised in Ghana until the age of 14 when she moved to the United Kingdom. She completed her secondary schooling there and joined University of Cambridge for her BA and MA in Modern Languages and MPhil in Latin-American Studies. She returned to Ghana in 1992 where she works as a freelance consultant on development issues while raising two daughters. She took up fiction writing in the late 1990s and has since published several short stories in various anthologies and journals across Africa, in the UK and the US and is now working on a novel. She was nominated for the 2009 Caine Prize and the 2011 Burt Award for children's writing. Mamle combines her work and writing with raising her two lovely children.

Beatrice Lamwaka was a finalist for the 2011 Caine Prize and the 2009 SA PEN/ Studzinski Literary Award and was a fellow at the Harry Frank Guggenheim Foundation/African Institute of South Africa Young Scholars Programme in 2009. Her stories have been published

181

in national and international journals and anthologies. She is currently working on her first novel and a compilation of short stories. She is the Treasurer, Uganda Women Writers Association (FEMRITE).

Elieshi Lema is an author and a publisher based in Dar-es-Salaam, Tanzania. She has published 14 children's books and two novels. Her first novel, Parched Earth, won the Best Book Award in 2001 and in 2002 received an honorary mention from the NOMA award committee, who called it "perhaps the first feminist Tanzanian novel in English." It was later translated into Swedish by Tranan Publishers, Sweden. Her second novel, In the Belly of Dar-es-Salaam, was shortlisted for the Burt Award for African Literature in 2010. She is the Director of E & D Vision Publishing and founder member of the Children's Book Project, Tanzania. She was also Eastern Africa Regional Director of CODE - Canadian Organisation for Development. She is passionate about availing young people with books and is an advocate for girls' and women's rights.

Elizabeth Namakula Lenana, who has a BA in Mass Communication from Makerere University, is an upcoming Ugandan writer with articles published in the Sunday Vision newspaper and Start, an arts journal. She has a few unpublished novels.

182

Kerstin Norborg was born in 1961, grew up in southern Sweden, and now lives in Stockholm. She works as a writing teacher at Öland's Folk High School and has previously worked as a journalist and a theatre musician. She started her literary career as a poet with the collection Vakenlandet (1994) and in 2001 published her first novel, Min Faders Hus, which was nominated for the August Prize. She has also published Så Fort Jag Går Ut (1998), Min Faders Hus (2001), Missed Abortion (2005), and I Will Never Know If She Hears (2009).

Constance Obonyo is a Ugandan writer with a law degree from the University of Buckingham, UK. Her short stories and poems have been published in several FEMRITE anthologies and she has contributed articles to various newspapers and magazines. She is a nominee for the 2011 Commonwealth Short Story Prize.

Maliya Mzyece Sililo was born in 1952 in Eastern Province, Zambia. She teaches English as a Foreign Language at Evelyn Hone College, Lusaka, on a part-time basis. She is a retired head teacher who has taught at all levels from primary schools to tertiary institutions. She holds a BA degree in Education and is currently

183

studying for a Masters in Literacy and Learning at the University of Zambia. Her published work includes a novella, Picking up the Pieces. She has also published poems and is an established story teller.

Lillian Tindyebwa has an MA in Literature from Makerere University. She is a founder member of the Uganda Women Writers Association (FEMRITE) and has published short stories in the following anthologies: A Woman's Voice, Words from a Granary, I Dare to Say, Beyond the Dance, Talking Tales, and Never Too Late. Her first novel, Recipe for Disaster, was published by Fountain Publishers, and her children's stories, A Time to Remember, Maggie's Friends, and A Will to Win are published by Macmillan. She is a lecturer of Literature and Linguistics at Kabale University in South Western Uganda and is working on a novel entitled, Dancing Together.

Hilda Twongyeirwe is a founder member of the Uganda Women Writers Association (FEMRITE). She has published short stories and poems in anthologies and co-edited literary works. Another Anthology she has edited with Lawrence Hill Books, Chicago will come out in Early 2012. In 2008, she was awarded the National Book Trust of Uganda Certificate of Recognition for her outstanding contribution to children's literature for her book, Fina the Dancer. She has also published children's books in her mother tongue,

184

Rukiga-Runyankore, courtesy of Longhorn Publishers. She is a member of the Banyakigezi International Community, Uganda Chapter and a member of the panel of Judges for Sustainable Tourism Media Awards in Uganda. She holds a MA in Public Administration and Management and a BA in Social Sciences from Makerere University and a diploma in Education. She is the Coordinator of FEMRITE.

Birgitta Wallin was born in 1962 in Sala, Sweden and now lives in Stockholm. She is the chief editor of Karavan, a quarterly that focuses on literature from Africa, Asia and Latin America. She has also been deeply involved in an Indo-Swedish Translation Project and has edited several anthologies. As a translator from English to Swedish, she has just finished work on a second novel, Brixton Beach, by Roma Tearne.

Ayeta Anne Wangusa, born in Kampala, Uganda in 1971, is a founding member of FEMRITE, which published her first novel, Memoirs of a Mother, in 1998. She is also a founding member of the African Writers Trust and is on its advisory board. She has attended the International Writers Programme at the University of Iowa; the Cheltenham Literature Festival, UK; has served on the steering committee of Women Writing Africa, Eastern Africa project of the Feminist Press (New York); and was a judge of the Commonwealth Writers Prize for the African Region in 2003. In addition to her literary career, she has a parallel career

185

in social development, governance, and women's rights. She holds a BA in Literature and Sociology and a MA in Literature, both from Makerere University, and a MA in New Media, Governance and Democracy, from the University of Leicester, UK. She lives in Arusha, Tanzania.

Molara Wood won the inaugural John La Rose Memorial Short Story Competition. Her work has been published internationally in journals including Sable Litmag, Farafina, Chimurenga, Per Contra and African Literature Today. Her fiction is also featured in the following anthologies: One World, A Life in Full (2010 Caine Prize Anthology) and The New Gong Book of New Nigerian Short Stories. She lives in Lagos, where she works as the Arts and Culture Editor of a national newspaper.

Other Publications by Femrite

Publication   Author/Editor

Anthologies:

A Woman's Voice (1998); *Mary K. Okurut / Violet Barungi*
Words From A Granary (1998) - *Violet Barungi*
Gifts of Harvest (2006); *Violet Barungi*
Pumpkin Seeds and Other Gifts (2009); *Helen Moffet / Violet Barungi*
Talking Tales   (2009); *Violet Barungi*
Never Too Late (2011); *Hilda Twongyeirwe / Aaron Mushengyezi*

True Life Stories:

Tears of Hope   (2003); *Violet Barungi*
I Dare To Say (2007); *Dr. Susan Kiguli / Violet Barungi*
Today You Will Understand(2008); *Jackie Christie*
Farming Ashes (2009); *Hilda Twongyeirwe / Violet Barungi*
Beyond the Dance (2009); *Violet Barungi / Hilda Twongyeirwe*

Novels:

Memoirs of a Mother (1998); *Ayeta Anne Wangusa*
The Invisible Weevil (1998); *Mary K. Okurut*
Silent Patience(1999); *Jane Kaberuka*
A Season of Mirth (2001); *Regina Amollo*
Secrets No More (1999); *Goretti Kyomuhendo*
Cassandra (1999); *Violet Barungi*
Shockwaves Across the Ocean (2005); *Bananuka Jocelyn Ekochu*
Poetry:

The African Saga (1998); *Susan Kiguli*
No Hearts At home (1999); *Christine Oryema Lalobo*

Painted Voices vol. I (2008); *FEMRITE writers*
Painted Voices vol. II (2009); *FEMRITE writers*
The Butterfly Dance (2010); *Rose Rwakasisi / Okaka Dokotum*

Others

In Their Own Words (2006); *Violet Barungi*
Directory of Ugandan Writers (2000); *Benard Tabaire*
5booklets - Where There's No Doctor(2000); *Violet Barungi*